ENGLISH FOLK TALES OF COAST AND SEA

ENGLISH FOLK TALES OF COAST AND SEA

LISA SCHNEIDAU

The History Press

For my brother Karl Schneidau,
who was usually first to see the sea
with love

First published 2024

The History Press
97 St George's Place, Cheltenham,
Gloucestershire, GL50 3QB
www.thehistorypress.co.uk

British Library Cataloguing in Publication Data.
A catalogue record for this book is available from the British Library.

ISBN 978 1 80399 423 9

Typesetting and origination by The History Press.
Printed and bound in Great Britain by TJ Books Limited, Padstow, Cornwall.

FSC www.fsc.org MIX Paper | Supporting responsible forestry FSC® C013056

Trees for Life

CONTENTS

ABOUT THE AUTHOR

Lisa Schneidau is a professional storyteller. She tells traditional and contemporary stories that inspire, provoke curiosity, and build stronger connections between people and nature.

Lisa trained as an ecologist. She has worked with wildlife charities all over Britain to restore nature in the landscape, in roles including farm advisor, river surveyor, political lobbyist and conservation director. She lives on Dartmoor.

Lisa is the author of the following The History Press titles:

Botanical Folk Tales of Britain and Ireland (2018)
Woodland Folk Tales of Britain and Ireland (2020)
River Folk Tales of Britain and Ireland (2022)

PRAISE FOR *ENGLISH FOLK TALES OF COAST AND SEA*

'Lisa Schneidau has an environmentalist's eye and a storyteller's heart, weaving together both precision and passion in this utterly engaging new collection of seafaring stories. Schneidau has dived deep into the ocean of folk tales and legends from every corner of coastal England, pulling up a treasure hoard of shimmering stories that deserve to be shared widely. A few of the tales I was aware of, but many were brand new to me – a testament to her diligence and delight in researching the source material. As someone who lives by the sea, this feels like a book to be dipped into often and enjoyed as much as the salty sea itself.'

Martin Maudsley, storyteller and author.

'This delightful book is filled with fascinating and enchanting folklore and histories of both coast and sea. Even if you are not a coastal dweller, you will find magic and wonder in some of England's oldest and strangest tales. A lovely read.'

Annie Worsely, author and blogger.

ACKNOWLEDGEMENTS

Where possible, I have drawn on multiple story sources for every traditional story retold here. I'm grateful to the folklorists and authors whose research has heavily influenced this book, especially Katherine Briggs, Sophia Kingshill, Ruth Tongue and Jennifer Westwood.

My thanks to the ever generous and wondrous storytelling community; the audiences and school classes who have listened and shared the stories and given feedback; and all the storytellers who have collected and shared these tales in the telling down the generations. I hope I have honoured their stories well here and added something useful to the tradition.

Thanks to David Wyatt for his beautiful cover artwork, and to Nicola Guy at The History Press for all her support in bringing the book together.

Thanks in particular to Annelies Acda, Cornish National Music Archive, Simon Dell, Earl Fontainelle, Moira Houghton, Sara Hurley, Caroline Preston, Holly Schneidau, Karl Schneidau, Beccy Swaine, Jo Swift, Tina Thomas and Nikki Walsh; and to Tony Whitehead, who has provided support, encouragement and inspiration throughout.

INTRODUCTION

So the first land we made, it is called the Deadman
Then Ram Head off Plymouth, Start, Portland and Wight
We sailed then by Beachy, by Fairlight and Dungeness
And then bore away for the South Foreland light

We'll rant and we'll roar, like true British sailors
We'll rant and we'll roar, all on the salt seas
Until we strike soundings in the channel of old England
From Ushant to Scilly 'tis thirty-five leagues

Traditional English folk song

There's a picture of my brother and I on the seafront at Lyme Regis in Dorset. I am about 3 years old, running ahead in a swimming costume. My little legs are rolls of bronzed puppy fat. What's left of the ice cream in my hand is plastered all over my face. I'm looking pretty determined, wherever I'm going, and my big brother Karl looks the picture of happiness.

The photo was taken in 1974. We Buckinghamshire landlubbers went to the south coast every year, and we loved Lyme. Past the ice cream shop and the amusement arcade (both of which are still there), I didn't know at the time that I was being introduced to thousands, if not millions, of years of English marine stories.

We learned of the local pioneer and palaeontologist Mary Anning. A century and a half earlier, she found fossils at Lyme Regis that advanced our knowledge of evolution and ancient creatures. We kicked around the bottom of the cliffs, looking for our own fossil treasures, and clambered over the walls that stopped the beach from eroding. We skipped along the Cobb, tried not to slip on the rocks, popped all the bladder wrack we could find, and wondered at the sea anemones waving their pink tentacles in the rock pools. We fished for darting prawns and yellow periwinkles, and Grandma boiled them up for a feast when we got back to the cottage (the smell of vinegar and prawns still takes me back there). At night, we gazed out from our Enid Blyton-esque Faraway House and saw the lights of great tankers far out in Lyme Bay. They seemed very different to the ancient ships and wrecks we had heard stories about.

Lyme Regis is one version of the English coastline and, fifty years on, this little girl has been lucky enough to experience many others. England's 2,748 miles of coastline includes the pebbles and pier of Brighton, the sublime beauty of the Farne Islands, the unforgiving rocks of north Devon, miles of broad sand in Norfolk, the endless mud of the Severn estuary in Somerset, tiny coves and crashing waves in Cornwall, the white cliffs at Dover, the sand and mudflats of Morecambe Bay and the bustling ports of Southampton, Hull and Liverpool, not to mention the Thames estuary. Although nobody in England lives more than 70 miles from the sea, those who live on the coast somehow have quite different perspectives from those inland. They breathe the salt air, and live side by side with the endless possibility of the ocean.

I trained as an ecologist, encouraged to look for nature in any place and to question why it's there and how it's influenced by human activity. Now I work as a storyteller, I find myself looking at England's coasts and seas with very different eyes. Here at the edge of our country, where the land meets the great unknown ocean, is a place of dissolution, adventure and extremes. That goes for people as well as nature, and it's reflected in our culture and traditions.

Folk tales are the local stories that become part of our heritage, handed on from person to person, often through telling in the oral tradition rather than writing. They talk of human experience, wisdom and interaction with our environment: little snippets of life where things happen, with a beginning, a middle and an end. We don't know how old many of our folk tales actually are, or who first told them, but they might be hundreds or even thousands of years old. New folk tales are still being created, and we have no idea which ones will stand the test of time, or how otherworldly and imaginative they may become.

Here are fifty-two folk tales from the coasts and seas of England. I am in the good company of other storytellers from Wales (Peter Stevenson), Scotland (Tom Muir) and Ireland (Colin Urwin) who have written separate volumes with The History Press on marine folk tales for their respective countries. My own volume includes a couple of stories from the Isle of Man, an independent island, to ensure its colourful folklore is represented between us.

These are my own versions of traditional folk tales. I have chosen stories that I particularly enjoy, that cover the wide geography of England's coasts, and that I feel resonate with our natural history and our heritage. I have told many of these tales to different audiences, indoors and out in nature, sharing ideas and emotions that the stories provoke. They are stories for all ages, although some are darker than others, and the teller will need to decide which stories to share with very young ones.

I have hunted out stories from many different sources: folklore archives and collections; natural history literature; and, of course, listening to storytellers. Some tales are well known, others more obscure. Like all storytellers, I am grateful to those who have collected and told these stories all down the generations, known and unknown. Wherever possible, I have tried to pursue a story back to its oldest referenced source. A list of story sources and further reading is provided.

The folk tales in this book are presented in chapters according to their subject. More than any other stories of our environment, I have found that England's marine and coastal folk tales often deal with death as a matter of fact part of life. Many are embellished true stories of extraordinary events in desperate times. The challenges presented in these stories are sometimes human-created (such as smuggling, inequality, taxes and war), and sometimes nature-created (storms and mists). Yet many of these folk tales also speak to the wonder of the more than human natural world on our coasts and out at sea, and here we find shapeshifting birds, mermaids, magical fish and sea-dragons. I will leave it up to you to decide how much these characters represent the interface between humans and nature – the magic of life where nature cannot speak for itself – and how much they might be real!

Folk tales have many loose ends and inconclusive endings, as they represent fragments of experience that have been handed down to us by luck or chance. They might be short or abrupt. They also represent the messy business of the human condition, which may or may not include happy endings. Working with folk tales involves listening and letting the stories work on you – not deciding what you would like to be told.

This book has been written as a resource to be used for storytelling about our natural world. My aim is to bring our folk tale heritage to a wider audience. The stories provoke curiosity about England's relationship with our coasts and seas through the centuries, our marine wildlife and our own wild oceanic imaginings.

There's another important reason for sharing these stories. England's relationship with the sea is changing rapidly, as the planet warms and climate chaos increases. Our marine wildlife is in crisis from over-exploitation and pollution. The next few decades will bring coastal challenges beyond any we have ever known. I believe the old tales hold wisdom for us: about the resourcefulness of the English people in times of change; about the values that will help to see us through difficult days; and about the wonders of nature that we must not take for granted. In a time when so much of human discourse isn't based on anything real at all, our folk tales are a good way to reconnect with the emotions and realities of place.

So, even better than reading the stories, do tell them to others – in your own words, not mine. That is the way that stories change, and grow, and stay alive year on year.

I hope you have as much fun reading and telling these stories as I have had in working with them. Let the tide nibble at your toes now. The sea and its stories are waiting.

1

SONG OF THE SIREN

One Friday morn as we'd set sail,
And our ship not far from land,
We there did espy a fair mermaid,
With a comb and a glass in her hand…

Child Ballad no. 289 'The Mermaid'

On a July night in 1825 or 1826, when the full moon was high in the sky over Bude, young Robert Hawker was bored. So he swam out to a rock a little way from the shore, wrapped an oilskin round his legs, plaited a wig for himself out of seaweed, and began to flash light from the moon with a small hand mirror. Presently he began to croon, and then keened to the heavens with a high-pitched wail.

The good people of Bude ran out to see this wonder of the sea. 'It's a merry-maid!' they whispered to one another. Soon, and most mysteriously, the sea-siren jumped off the rocks, into the sea, and was gone from sight.

The next evening, the crowds were there before the mermaid, but eventually she reappeared, combing her tresses and singing a desolate song. Military telescopes were fetched to observe the entrancing creature.

This continued for several nights, until one keen watcher observed the mermaid was shivering with cold. The singing died away, then they heard the mermaid bellow 'God Save The King!' in a fine baritone; then the creature disappeared into the water, never to be seen again.

Not all mermaid stories are as obvious or eccentric as this little Baring-Gould anecdote. Many people who have spent time on the coasts and beaches of England will swear they have seen an actual mermaid (a creature with a human body and the tail of a fish), or a fish-creature, or a wild man who lives in the sea.

Mermaids and their equivalents are a worldwide folklore motif, perhaps influenced by early Greek stories of sirens. Sometimes they appear in stories at times of great danger or bad omen, but sometimes they will offer protection or gifts to humankind. One early Celtic text describes a mermaid cast up by the sea in AD 887 that was 160ft long with both fingers and nose measuring 7ft long. Among the earliest images of a mermaid in England is in the Norman chapel of Durham Castle, dated to 1078.

Mermaid folk tales and ballads are found all over the British Isles, but are particularly common in the south-west of England. A sea-morgan is a related sea creature, of Celtic and Breton origin, that lures people to their death in the sea. Both mermaids and sea-morgans are quite different to the selkie (seal-people) stories of Celtic and Norse origin, mostly found in Scotland and Ireland.

There is something seductive about mermaids, real or otherwise, that makes us want to dissolve into them; something about the merging of human and fish that conveys a magical allure. They speak of the deep mystery of the ocean, and the mortal dangers of living more with the sea than with the land.

The Droll of the Mermaid

The story of Lutey and the Mermaid is one of the classic Cornish folk tales. When William Bottrell recorded it in 1870, he heard it from one of the last Cornish droll-tellers.

'Uncle' Anthony James was blind and relied on his dog and a young lad to guide him about with his stories and his fiddle. He related tall tales (or drolls) of the Lutey family of Cury, who were famously conjurers and white witches after one of their ancestors found a stranded mermaid on the shore.

Robert Hunt recorded a different take on the story in his Popular Romances of the West of England *in 1881, probably also sourced from Bottrell, ending with the warning 'Sceptical people are never lovable people.' I have combined both Bottrell's and Hunt's versions into my own take on the story.*

This folk tale is often told in a way that mocks Lutey as a country simpleton enchanted by beauty. I think there's a little more to the story than that. Liz Greene, mythologist and astrologer, has mused that Lutey is under a classic Neptunian spell from the mermaid, one of the sacred female water spirits of the ancients.

Mermaids offer the promise of redemption and perfection, becoming one with the divine, all submerged in the mysterious depths of the ocean. Yet there is healing available to those who dare to dream. Lutey and his family are given that great gift as well.

Many years ago, a man called Lutey lived with his wife, Ann Betty, in a little stone cottage near the shore at Cury (that used to be known as Corantyn), on the Lizard. Their children were grown up and gone, and so the two of them survived from a bit of Lutey's fishing, and a bit of his wife's growing crops and storing, and a bit of taking whatever plunder washed up on the shore from any boats coming to grief on the rocks at Lizard Point.

It was a simple life, and they made the best of it. But after the practical work of the day was done, Lutey loved to wander the sands and think deeply about life, gazing on the rolling ocean and dreaming about what might lie beyond.

That particular year had been hard on the whole village. Disease was rife, and Lutey's wife was recovering from a bad illness. One summer's evening, Lutey had finished cutting the turf and wandered down to the beach towards a little cove. It was a shimmering evening, as the light played tricks on the deep blue water far away. The tide was out and the sands were scattered with pools and rocks, their barnacles and limpets sealed tight against the heat. Gulls cried overheard and the peep of the oystercatcher punctuated the sky – but here was a different sound. It was a sad cry, half-sobbing, a child in distress. This was not a bird of any kind, and it came from the shore in front of him.

Lutey crept towards the sound, his feet silent on wet sand. There was a tall rock in front of him, and he peered around it to the large rock pool behind.

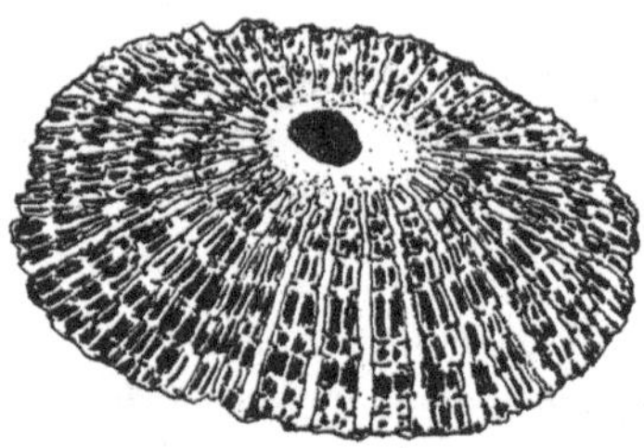

There in the water was a vision of sweetness. She had flowing pale hair that spread out on the water of the pool and mingled with the seaweed. Her shell-like skin gleamed in the sun as her face tilted towards the ocean with longing, her eyes mournful and swollen from crying.

Lutey hardly dared to breathe. A merry-maid! He had heard stories, of course, and he had heard them singing in the moonlight far away, but he had never seen one this close!

The mermaid sensed Lutey's gaze, gave a little cry and dived into the water to hide.

'Don't be afraid,' crooned Lutey in a low voice to the mass of hair and bladder wrack and glittering silver scales under the water. 'Don't worry, I won't hurt you. Truth is, I'm just as frightened as you are. Come out, you're safe.'

Gradually, the mermaid emerged from the pool into the air again, crying bitterly, and sat on the rocky edge with her tail-fin still tucked in the water.

'Now then, maid,' said Lutey, 'I don't know if you can understand my mumblings, but I'd dearly like to know why you're crying.'

The mermaid wiped her face clear and looked Lutey straight in the eyes. He gave a start at that, for her eyes were deep sapphire blue, the colour of the wide ocean beyond the rocks: water you could lose yourself in.

She sighed. 'I'm stranded,' she said. 'Only three hours ago, I left my husband and children happily snoozing, surrounded by sea flowers, basking in the sunlit waters. I had a mind to catch their supper, and I was also curious about the human places here on the coast. So I swam a little too far in, and I was so taken up with chasing the shrimps and dancing with the sea wrack, that I didn't notice I was stranded until it was too late!' She fell to snivelling again, building up to proper crying.

Lutey hurriedly interrupted. 'Surely you can wait until the tide comes back in again, then go to join them? I can keep you company in the meantime.'

'No, that won't work,' she said between sobs. 'My husband will wake up soon, hungry, and look for his supper. If I don't bring him the food he needs, he's sure to eat up some of our pretty children … I still haven't recovered from last time it happened!'

'Surely he wouldn't do that!' said Lutey.

'He's very jealous too, goodness knows what he would do to me,' she insisted. 'Please, help me get back to the sea!'

Now Lutey was in a fix. He had heard many stories about mermaids. People said that you should never offend a mermaid, for if they were angry there was no knowing what they'd do. But people also said it was dangerous to get too close to a mermaid.

Now he was here with an actual live mermaid, Lutey could see that people didn't understand. This creature wasn't dangerous or angry. She was sweet and sensitive and vulnerable. She was more beautiful than any mortal woman he had ever seen. What was the harm in helping?

'Carry me to the sea,' she pleaded. 'It will only be a few minutes of your time, and I will give you fine gifts. I'll give you anything you wish for.' Her eyes were huge now, emerald-green pools glittering in the evening sunlight.

Lutey reached forward, put one arm around her shining silver scales and another round her waist. He lifted the mermaid up, finding her surprisingly heavy. The mermaid immediately put her arms around his neck and snuggled into his warmth.

'What is it that you wish for? Is it to be gold, silver or jewels?'

Now Lutey's mind was blank for any idea of gifts, for his mind was full of her. He looked back and saw his little stone cottage in the distance, and with difficulty recalled his life with his wife and the people of the village.

'Gold and silver aren't much use to us here,' said Lutey slowly. 'But good health, that's a different matter … the power to charm away disease and difficulty would be a fine thing.'

She looked at him pointedly. 'You're a good man,' she said. 'It shall be done, and you and your family will be provided for all your days. But I will give you another gift.'

She held out a gleaming comb made of pearl. 'Take this,' she said, 'it will prove to you that you have not been dreaming. Whenever you need me, comb the sea three times with this, and I will come to your help. Now – take me to the sea.'

He carried the mermaid down the beach towards the tide, walking with some difficulty as the sand got wetter and his burden got heavier. Soon the waves were washing over his shoes and he began to wade out to sea, but he didn't let go of the mermaid.

'Lutey,' she whispered in his ear, 'come with me. Come with me to our place under the sea.'

Lutey's mind was swirling into eddies, looping and drifting with the tide, but he did not reply; he gazed out to the waves as he waded deeper, still holding her tight.

The water was up to his knees now. She whispered again, using deliberate words as if chanting a spell. 'Lutey. It is so beautiful in our place under the sea. There are all the things you would wish for: fine food, the best of rum, and many sparkling sea-women just like me. There are sea creatures of all colours, wondrous to behold. I will make you gills so you can breathe with us and live with us, be like us, the sea-people, at one with the deep ocean.'

The water was up to his waist now. Lutey's eyes were glazed and his mind addled, as the water lapped around him and the sea currents tugged at his legs, and still he would not let go of the mermaid.

Then, among the alarm cries of the gulls, a different sound, distant at first, but insistent and louder: a familiar noise. It was Lutey's dog, standing on the shore, barking and barking for all it was worth.

Lutey blinked, and tried to drop the mermaid, but she clung on to him. 'Lutey–'

'No … maid, I will NOT come with you!' Lutey wrenched an arm free and reached down to his belt for his knife. 'I'll have none of your enchantments or your cunning. Go back to the sea!' As Lutey managed to brandish his sailor's knife in the air, the mermaid let go and her golden hair spread out in the water again.

She turned to him, her eyes dark. 'Nine years, my love! Nine of your human years, and I will return for you.' There was a flick of a silver tail, then she was gone.

Lutey's heart was pounding in his chest as he half-swam, half-waded back to shore, spitting out gulpfuls of salt water. The faithful dog followed Lutey up from the shore until he reached a little cave at the back of the beach. This was the place where Lutey stored a few smuggled treats, including brandy. He found the bottle he was looking for, tugged at the cork and drank deep of the contents, as the brandy warmed his belly and soothed his senses.

Ann Betty Lutey was worried. Her husband hadn't come home, and she had watched for him all night. When the dawn broke, she wandered down to the beach, to the little cave she wasn't supposed to know about.

There was her beloved husband, fast asleep against some old sails and snoring. Ann Betty aimed a swift kick at his buttock.

Lutey stirred. 'What … Who are you … where am I? Am I at the bottom of the sea, my beauty?'

Another kick. 'I'm your wife, as you know full well, and you've not called me beauty in twenty-five years,' she said. 'Get up, you old scoundrel, you've got some explaining to do over breakfast.'

Lutey followed his wife sheepishly along the beach to their little cottage, and over a hearty breakfast – which made him feel much better – he told her everything he could remember.

'She even gave me a pearly comb to prove it wasn't a dream … look!' He brought it out of his pocket triumphantly.

'That's no comb,' said Ann Betty. 'That's an old shark's jaw full of teeth. You old fool.'

Nevertheless, the story was a good one. Although Ann Betty was sworn to secrecy for fear of Lutey looking foolish, the story of the mermaid and the gifts she had given to Lutey spread through the little village of Cury like seeping seawater. There was no doubt that, since the mermaid was found, Ann Betty was feeling in better health than she had done for months.

A couple of days later, there was a knock at the door. It was an old woman carrying a young child. 'Please,' she said. 'I've heard you've got the gift of healing in this house. My granddaughter has been running a high fever for a day and a night. Can you cure her?'

Lutey discovered that his wish had been granted. He could heal the sick and undo evil magic, and no matter where he went in Cornwall or beyond, he was hailed as a hero. He never charged for helping people, and somehow his family were always well clothed and well fed.

Nine years later, Lutey had completely forgotten about the mermaid. Life was good. One night in high summer, he and a friend went out one evening in Lutey's little fishing boat, and they went for the edge of the shore just beyond the rocks.

There wasn't a breath of wind that night, and the sea was almost still, caressed by tiny ripples, as the men chatted. Then, as if from nowhere, a wind whipped up along the water. The little boat was soon lurching dangerously on high waves, both men trying to keep afloat – yet the sky was still clear.

A huge wave rolled towards them then, crested with sea foam, and in the middle of the sea foam rode the mermaid, her arms outstretched and her sparkling eyes fixed on Lutey.

As if bewitched, Lutey stood up in the rocking boat and turned towards the deep ocean. 'It's time,' he said, and took one step off the edge of the boat, despite his friend's attempts to stop him.

Lutey's friend peered down into the water, and for a moment he saw Lutey and the mermaid in each other's arms, her silver scales sparkling and their hair mingling in the water. Then they were gone. The water was still again, and Lutey's friend was left alone in his little boat under the summer moon.

Lutey was never seen again in the village of Cury. His children and grandchildren held and used the same healing powers, as they do to this day.

But every nine years, a member of the Lutey family is always lost at sea.

Sea-Morgans and Mud

The Somerset coast is of a different character altogether, compared with the rest of south-west England. It is part of the great Severn Estuary, or 'Severn Sea', which boasts a tidal range of 13m – the second highest tidal range in the world – along with the famous Severn Bore. From the cliffs off Exmoor to the rocky shore at Kilve, round Bridgwater Bay to Weston-super-Mare and up towards Clevedon, with some beautiful beaches but mostly mud, this part of the English coastline has a character that is oozing, endless and slow. But it's deceptive: this is a dangerous place, and the muddy estuary water holds strong currents. Walk too far out at low tide, and you can easily disappear in the quicksand.

As ever, people have found ways to cope: mud-horses are wooden sledges pushed in front by the fisherman to safely carry the fish and shrimps from their nets across the mudflats to the shore. 'Glatting' or 'congering' is hunting for conger eels with dogs at low tide, seeking out the places where the submerged eels are hiding and waiting for the water to come back in. Conger eels occur in the sea all around the British Isles, and they can be huge – several metres long and up to about 250lb in weight. These strong, ferocious fish will give a nasty bite. Mature adults will spawn once and then die, which makes conger eels vulnerable to over-fishing.

The Somerset coastline hosts more contemporary weirdness thanks to the Hinkley B and C power stations, which are visible from most high places in the county. Nearby Steart Point is among the first places in the south-west of England where land will be lost to the sea in the next few years due to climate change and the rising of sea levels. Steart is being managed by the Wildfowl and Wetlands Trust and Environment Agency to create new salt marsh and freshwater wetland, 'managing' the advance of the sea with the input of local people.

Ruth Tongue recorded folk tales about sea-morgans from this part of the coast. These are water spirits who delight in drowning humans. Similar spirits are found in Welsh and Breton folklore. I love the spirit of these little stories, cheating the supernatural wherever possible to make sure of a good catch. The first story is from Steart, the second from Watchet, and the third from Berrow, where the islands Steep Holm and Flat Holm loom from the sea. The last story may refer to an angler fish.

Everyone knew about the sea-morgan who would sing so beautifully in the autumn time. People would go to hear her, and those who came back said she had a beautiful face as well as a beautiful voice. But those who waded out too far didn't come back. They were lured into the sea-morgan's clutches by her song-spell, or taken down by the quicksand. The conger eels got a slap-up feast on those days. It wasn't a good way to meet your maker.

One woman who lived nearby had a son who was deaf, and so she reckoned it would be safe for him to go and get rid of the sea-morgan, as he wouldn't be able to hear the deadly song.

The lad got close enough to see the morgan. She had her mouth open wide, crooning away. 'Yuk,' he thought, 'her hair's all green!' So, he got his mud-horse, and went out over the flats with his eel-spear ready to strike at the morgan. But he got distracted very easily: there were so many eels about. All the time she was singing, he got a good catch of eels, and he didn't sink in the quicksand because of the mud-horse.

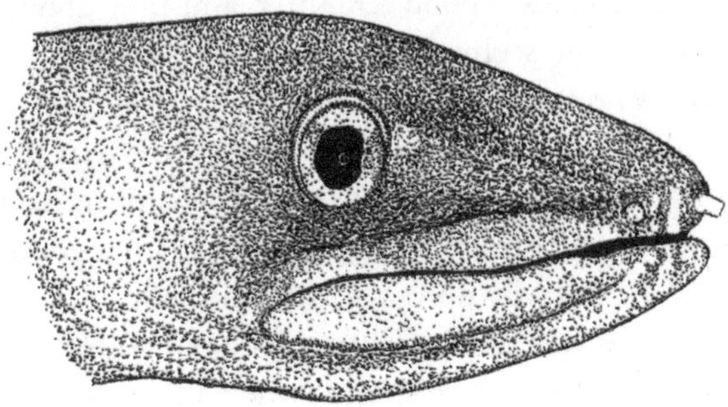

After he'd got twelve of those big fat conger eels, the sea-morgan gave a shriek and disappeared. She was never seen again.

Everyone in Steart had conger eel pie that week, and a lot of it.

A fisherman heard a sea-morgan singing in the dimpsey time on the beach at St Audrie's Bay. But he wasn't the quietest of people, crunching through the stones and pebbles, and the sea-morgans heard him a mile off. They scurried away, but they left one of their little babies behind, crying and kicking underneath the waterfall at the bottom of the cliff.

The fisherman hurried to the child and picked her up. She tugged at his heartstrings there and then. It hadn't been long since he had to bury his own baby daughter in Watchet churchyard, and his wife was drowning in grief. So, he saw the tiny sea-morgan child as a gift sent from Heaven, and he took her home to fill the empty cradle.

His wife was delighted, and loved the little girl at once. But she could never get the baby's hair dry, no matter how much she messed it with a towel, or how much sunlight the child had; her hair would always be drenched with salt water.

The little girl grew up quickly, as they do, and was toddling around before long, always drawn to the streams and the ponds in the village. She made a good daughter, and they grew so used to her that everything seemed all right – until one day a neighbour came into the house.

'Dear, dear,' said the neighbour to the little girl in that condescending way people sometimes talk to children, 'I saw you paddling in the stream – it isn't the right way for a good Christian girl to behave! And why don't you dry your hair?'

The girl's eyes were downcast to the floor, and her parents were trying to think of how to respond, when a low melody began to sound from the coast.

She looked up. 'They're singing my song. They want me. There will be a storm tonight.'

She ran upstairs at that, leaving her parents to try and explain. But it was no use. The meddling neighbour went and roused the official men of the village to chase out this little witch from their community.

But when the men arrived, the girl ran away laughing, and sent them off course, and teased them. 'Can't catch me!' She ran down towards the rocks and the sea, grey clouds gathering above her and the wind whipping up the sand. 'Can't catch me!' They heard her singing with joy by the old coast cart track as the gales howled.

Then a huge wave crashed over the road and took the little girl, and she was never seen again.

Off Berrow Sands, there was a huge fish with a huge mouth. It was such a huge fish that it used to swallow up all the other fish and all the sailors too – and what it didn't manage to eat, the conger eels finished off. In those days, the conger eels used to bark, and then everyone knew there was danger lurking in the deeper water.

This was no good for anyone, and one day a brave fisherman decided to sort it out.

He rowed out to the very big fish in his very small boat. The big fish opened its jaws ready to eat him up – but quick as a flash, he threw his anchor straight into the fish's mouth. The cold iron finished it off for good.

The Mermaid's Omen

A mermaid sighting, however alluring, is usually considered by sailors to be very bad luck, and even an omen of the wrecking or sinking of their ship. It's also considered very bad luck to sail on a Friday (see stories in Chapter 7).

This story is derived from a popular folk ballad, The Mermaid, *found all over England in broadsides and collections, together with a story that Ruth Tongue recorded from a Norfolk sailor in the 1940s. It tells of the bad omen of a mermaid, and the lament of men who risked their life at sea for their livelihoods, but were now fated to die in the waves.*

Two trawlers set off from Norfolk into the dark North Sea. The sailors weren't happy, because it was a Friday morning – and they really weren't happy, because they were ordered to sail past a place where the voices of shipwrecks could still be heard, near to their homes in Sheringham.

But the owner of the trawlers was a modern man, and he was having none of their superstitions. He was on board one of the trawlers, so the crew were polite to his face. But as they sailed near to the place of all the stories, all the crew of both trawlers were making all the prayers for safety they could think of.

They sailed north, a long way north, and into the waters around Scotland. The fishing was good, really good, but the seas were more dangerous than they'd been used to.

The further north they sailed, the higher the waves and the worse the conditions got. The owner of the trawlers laughed, enjoying his trip, and not wanting to lose face. The crew, still praying, worried the fishing was too good and that there was bad luck ahead.

Then, up ahead of them, a bit of wreckage drifted on the waves, and sitting on top of it was a lithe figure. In horror, the sailors realised that it had long green hair, like wrack, and it held a little mirror in one hand and a comb in the other.

The mermaid turned and looked directly at the sailors. None of them wanted to catch her gaze, but some of them just couldn't help it.

'Go closer,' called the owner. 'This is an amazing sight!' The men on his trawler didn't want to obey, of course, but their boat moved around the creature sitting on the wreck to get a better view, bad luck or no.

The captain of the other trawler managed to tear his gaze away from the beautiful creature. 'Turn and sail for harbour, quick as we can, boys!' he shouted. 'This is no place to be, if you want to live and see your sweetheart again.'

That trawler just made it safely in to harbour before a great storm blew up. By the time they got in, they'd lost most of their catch. But those sailors didn't care; they looked up at the moon's bright light after the storm had passed, and they thanked the lucky stars for their lives.

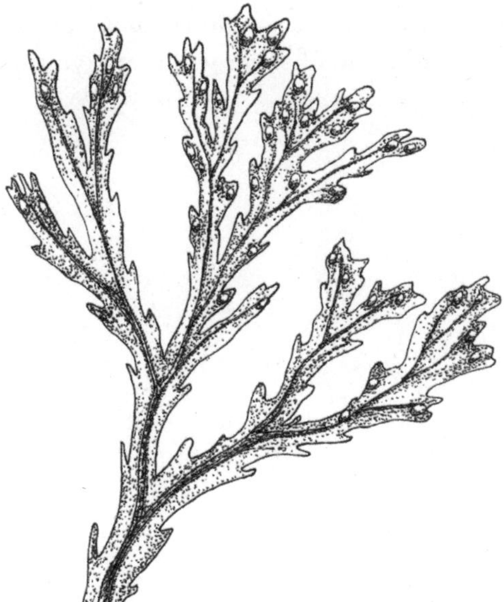

The owner's trawler, together with the owner and all its crew, was never seen again. Everyone reckoned it sank as soon as it touched that floating wreck it was circling. It was all the mermaid's fault, and all the sweethearts of the sailors back in Norfolk mourned for their lost loves, now at the bottom of the dark North Sea.

The following month, on a stormy Sunday morning, the good people of Sheringham were in church waiting for the service to begin. A man at the back spied a mermaid sitting quietly on the end of a pew.

'Get out! Get out!' he cried, 'we can't have the likes of you in here!' The mermaid was hurried out of the church and the door slammed behind her. Everyone tried to behave as if they hadn't seen anything unusual at all – because it was bad luck to have seen her.

At the end of the service, when everyone had left and nobody was looking, the little mermaid came back into the church and sat on the same end of the pew at the back of the church – where her likeness can still be seen today, carved in elm.

This story is one that you shouldn't tell, as it's bad luck to talk of fishermen, and none of them will thank you for it. So now you know.

The Mermaid of Zennor

At Zennor one sees infinite Atlantic, all peacock-mingled colours, and the gorse is sunshine itself.

D.H. Lawrence (1885–1930)
to J.M. Murray and K. Mansfield
4 February 1916

Here is one of the classic mermaid stories, which has been celebrated through poetry, film and theatre. It was originally recorded by William Bottrell in 1873. The mermaid carving in Zennor church is said to date from the fifteenth century.

Zennor is a small and pretty village on the northern coast of Cornwall, 14 miles from Land's End. It is blessed with much of historical interest, including Bronze Age field systems, burial chambers and barrows. The writer D.H. Lawrence lived here between 1915 and 1917 with his new wife Frieda; he finished writing Women in Love *but they had to leave due to accusations of spying.*

Young Matty Trewella, son of the warden of St Senara's church, was a fine-looking lad. He rang the church bells every Sunday without fail, and he sang in the choir – and what a voice he had! It was clear and loud as a bell.

'That voice would call in the angels,' said the old women of the village, 'he'd lure a mermaid with that voice.' The truth was, the good people of Zennor went along to church on a Sunday to hear Matty Trewella singing just as much as they wanted to commune with God. Who could blame them?

One particular Sunday, as they all dutifully shuffled into the pews of the little church and waited for the service to begin, there were whispers, and there were looks. A newcomer was sitting at the back of the church, just by the door. Who was she? She wasn't from Zennor, that was for sure.

She was young and slim, her face swathed in a veil so that nobody could see it properly, but her dress was a thing of dreams. The first Sunday she appeared, on a stormy February morning, her skirts had caught the lamplight with its gleams of angry greys and whites. The second time she appeared her dress swirled as she moved, teal and dark petrol. As the days grew longer in March and the birds were singing of the springtime, now the fabric peeping out from under the young woman's coat gleamed aquamarine and golden, like the sparkles of shallow waves as they met the shore.

She never spoke to anyone; she never raised her eyes or removed her veil. By the time the church service ended of a Sunday, people looked around and she had disappeared, slipping out of the church with nobody seeing, only to come in to the church again the next week.

Matty Trewella noticed her, of course, just like everyone else did: he could watch her from the choir while he was singing, although he pretended he wasn't looking. But as time went on, Matty couldn't drag his eyes away from the mysterious young woman. He found himself looking forward to seeing her every week, and when she was there in church, he was painfully aware of her presence, wherever he was.

Then it was Easter. The powerful tunes of Easter hymns, of death and resurrection, boomed through the little church accompanied by Matty's honeyed tones. There she was again at the back of the church, her dress glinting sapphire and azure in the coloured light that filtered through the church window.

Halfway through a particularly solemn hymn, Matty looked up and his song faltered. Her veil had slipped! Her eyes were looking straight at him, sparkling. At that moment, perhaps their hearts met across the church as well.

After that service, the mysterious woman disappeared again, and Matty Trewella was in a hurry. ''Scuse me.' He pushed past his fellow choristers and the villagers wanting to talk, and hurried out of the door of the church and down the road to the cliffs and the sea.

When, later that day, they called Matty for his Sunday lunch, there was no sign of him. He had vanished. After that, Matty's wonderful voice was never heard in the church again. The people of Zennor wondered whether he and the young woman had run off together. Many were sad at Matty's disappearance, and tutted at the scandalous notion of an elopement, but everyone wished them both well.

A few months later, a deep bell was heard sounding from the bay – unlike any sound the villagers had ever heard. It rang constantly, relentlessly, and it seemed to be coming from the waves themselves. The old people of the village thought it was the lost bell of Lyonesse, and just to be safe, the villagers boarded up their houses and shored up the boats.

Sure enough, the next day a violent storm arrived in Zennor. The precautions the villagers had put in place kept them all safe and sound, and minimised the damage that needed to be repaired afterwards.

Just as they were unlocking the doors and clearing up after the storm, a sea captain turned up in Zennor. 'I have news!' he shouted.

The villagers all followed him into the Tinner's Arms. The captain said, 'We were anchored about a mile out from Pendower Cove to see out the storm. But as the winds died down, there was a voice shouting out. I looked over the side and there was a young woman in the sea, with green eyes and pretty hair. I have to say – and here the captain looked around and lowered his voice – 'I couldn't see all of her, mind, but it looked like she wasn't wearing a scrap of clothing.'

The villagers nodded and tutted to each other. It was a mermaid, all right.

The captain continued. 'She asked me to shift – the anchor of our ship had landed on her home under the waves – and her husband was to come back from ringing the great bell in the bay, and he would want to see his wife and children safe.

'Well! I asked her if it was Matty Trewella, and she said 'Of course, he is my husband! But he doesn't forget where he comes from. Whenever there is a great storm on the way, he will ring the great bell of Lyonesse and warn everyone in Zennor, so they can be safe.'

The captain took another gulp from his jug of ale, and everyone nodded, well satisfied. 'So it seems like merry-maids aren't such bad luck for sailors after all.'

If you visit the little village of Zennor and go into St Senara's church, you will find a mermaid on the end of a wooden bench, carved in honour of that strange young woman who visited the church so long ago. The people of Zennor can still sleep soundly, even today, knowing that their friend Matty Trewella will always let them know if there is a storm on the way.

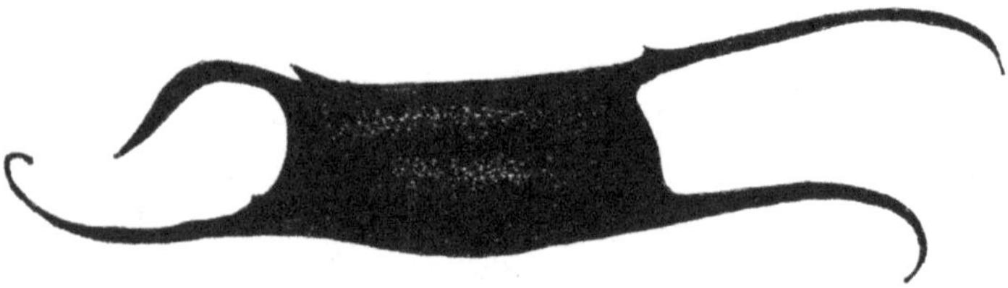

2

SAINTS AND SINNERS

Alone, alone, all, all alone,
Alone on a wide wide sea!
And never a saint took pity on
My soul in agony.

Samuel Taylor Coleridge, The Rime of the Ancient Mariner, *1798*

The sea is a place of wild extremes. It can be benign and wondrous and giving. Alternatively, in the words of Charles Dickens in *A Tale of Two Cities*, 'The sea did what it liked, and what it liked was destruction.' The transition from one state to the other can be swift.

No wonder so many folk tales from the English coast tell of the moral extremes represented by holy men, and Old Nick, the Devil himself. Both saints and devils are used to explain the existence of coastal formations or strange wonders. As the stories show, the dividing line between good and evil is not always a clear one.

THE HOLY ISLAND

The island of Lindisfarne, just off the Northumbrian coast, is a wildlife-rich jewel with a sacred and colourful heritage. The priory on Lindisfarne was founded in the year AD 634. The Viking raid on Lindisfarne in 793, deliberately targeting a holy place for the Christians, is considered to be the beginning of the 'Viking Age'. Even following the dissolution of the monasteries in the sixteenth century, and religious changes since that time, this 'Holy Island' remains a place of pilgrimage today for Christians and nature-lovers alike. The mudflats, dunes and rocky coast of Lindisfarne are designated as a National Nature Reserve to protect internationally important populations of wintering birds.

Eider ducks, common on the coast around Holy Island, are also known in Northumberland as Cuddy's duck, after St Cuthbert. Eider ducks are large, elegant birds that nest on the rocky shorelines of northern Britain. The males are black and white with a comical call, the females brown. Eider were economically valuable because of their soft feathers (eiderdowns were called this for a reason). Tradition says that Cuthbert was fond of eider ducks and issued formal orders for their protection on Lindisfarne.

Ravens, the largest of the crow family, are happily increasing their range again across the British Isles. Ravens have a long and dastardly folklore. They are said to be birds of ill omen and malevolent intent, as well as bringing protection. The collective noun for ravens is an 'unkindness' or a 'conspiracy'. I think their dark reputation is a pity, for the 'cronk-cronk' call and playful flight of the raven betrays a sharp intelligence and humour.

St Cuthbert (634–687) is an important Christian saint in the north of England and southern Scotland, and the patron saint of Northumbria. Cuthbert was bishop in both Lindisfarne and Melrose in Scotland. He travelled widely in his missionary work in these very early days for Christianity in the British Isles, and was well known for his generosity and wisdom; however, he lived a very austere and simple life, often as a hermit. His example has inspired people through the ages. Cuthbert's remains have now (hopefully) found their eternal rest at Durham Cathedral, following the long journeys described in these tales.

Bartholomew (died 1193) was a Benedictine hermit who received a vision of St Cuthbert and spent most of his life in seclusion at Lindisfarne Priory, newly restored at that time after the Norman conquest.

Eider ducks gather on the rocks in the springtime at Holy Island, fearing no humans. They build their nests everywhere, and everyone knows not to disturb them; the mothers lead their brown fluffy ducklings to the sea when they are very young.

Many years ago, a mother eider was leading her brood of little ones from the rocks to the sea, when one of the ducklings fell down into a great crevice in the rock. The mother stared in distress for a few moments, then turned and, bidding her children to stay, went to find the hermit Bartholomew.

She tugged at the hem of his cloak with her bill, and he got up, worried that he might be disturbing her nest. But she kept tugging at the cloth of his cloak, and he realised that the eider wanted for something. He followed her out to the rocks and when they got to the place where her little ones were still patiently standing, she pointed with her bill towards the crevice in the rock.

Peering down, Bartholomew could see the little bird with its wings outstretched, clinging on for dear life. He clambered down and rescued the little thing, of course, and the glint in the eider's eye showed she was pleased.

Then the mother eider continued on her way leading her brood down to the sea, and the hermit Bartholomew went back to his oratory.

One morning, Cuthbert noticed that the thatched roof of Lindisfarne Priory, made with love and toil by the holy men of the island, was being ripped apart. This crime was not committed by humans, but by two ravens who were seeking to make their own home from the thatch, and were merrily pulling out the straw and carrying it off as nesting material.

Cuthbert spoke sternly to the ravens, and asked them to collect their nest stuff from elsewhere on the island. Did they listen? Do ravens ever listen? 'Cronk, cronk,' they called out, like so much raven-laughter.

Cuthbert was not impressed. 'In the name of the Lord,' he cried, 'be off with you, and never return to this place that you have spoiled.'

The two birds bowed their heads, as if they had been dismally scolded, and then spread their great black wings and flew away.

Three days passed with no sign of the troublesome two. But towards the end of the third day, as Cuthbert was digging in the vegetable field, one of the ravens landed at a respectful distance, his bill bowed down to his claws and his mumbling croak muted and humble.

Cuthbert well understood the gesture, and gave the raven permission to return. It flew off, and soon returned with its mate, both of them carrying gifts: hunks of hog's lard, which Cuthbert graciously accepted.

For many years after that, the same ravens lived alongside the brethren of the priory on Holy Island, and neither party caused any annoyance to the other.

Cuthbert died after a painful illness. His body was buried on Lindisfarne on the same day, and everyone prayed for him to find eternal peace there.

Their wish was granted for over a hundred years, until the Norsemen came with their axes and their blades. For one day in early summer, holy blood ran in rivers and mingled with the salt water. The bodies of monks were trampled in the road like dung; others were taken as slaves. All the buildings of the priory were burned to the ground, and the holy treasures stolen.

Some monks had foreseen the great pagan terror and managed to escape. One of them had remembered the words of St Cuthbert: 'Rather than submit, I choose and wish that you take up my bones, fly from these places, and stay wherever God shall provide for you.'

Time was short. A wooden box was hurriedly made and the remains of the great saint were laid within it. Then, carrying the precious cargo, the monks fled the island to the mainland.

For seven long years, the monks travelled from place to place across the North Country. Sometimes they carried Cuthbert's coffin on their shoulders, and sometimes on a cart pulled by a horse. Always they travelled in fear of the Norsemen, and at one point they even tried to flee to Ireland, but a storm drove them back and they continued their journey in search of a place to find rest for the great saint.

One day they reached a hill not far from Chester-le-Street, and there the wagon carrying the coffin got stuck in deep mud. They tried yoking up more horses and even oxen to the cart, but nobody could shift it. Was this a sign that the good man wanted to stay?

For three days the monks fasted and prayed for guidance, and then one of them heard a voice from nowhere that said, 'Take the saint's body to Dunholm.'

'Where is Dunholm?' None of the monks had ever heard of the place.

Then a milkmaid passed by the cart, driving her cows home to milk. Another woman came by in the opposite direction, and called out to the first, 'Neighbour! Have you seen my dun cow with one short horn and one long? I have lost her.'

'Yes, I have,' came the reply, 'I saw her just now, wandering at Dunholm.'

The monks were excited at this. 'Please show us the way to this place of Dunholm.' They pulled the horse forward and tried to move the wagon one more time, and to their astonishment it came free and started to roll again, as if the axles of the wheels had been freshly greased.

Horse, cart, saint and monks followed the woman along the tracks and through the trees, to a beautiful, craggy place, surrounded by trees. When they looked down they could see the river twisting round and almost circling where they stood. This was the perfect place of protection. Next to the spot where the woman's short-horned dun cow stood, the monks fell to their knees and prayed that their journey had reached its end.

The monks laid the saint's bones to rest in the spot at Dunholm, and built a humble wooden church around the shrine for their beloved Cuthbert. The church was enlarged and improved over the years, until it became the great Durham Cathedral.

St Cuthbert's bones then found peace for a few hundred years, until yet another invasion of England. This time, William of Normandy had seized the land for himself, and all the English feared for their lives as any rebellion was staunched with sword and fire. The Harrying of the North had begun.

The monks at Durham feared for the sacred bones of Cuthbert, and hurriedly decided to take him back to Lindisfarne. On a bitingly cold day in December, Cuthbert's remains were disinterred and carried north and east to the coast, but when they came to the island crossing it was flooded by the tide.

They were trapped in an exposed place with no shelter, with temperatures below freezing and the night coming on. Many prayers and laments and cries for help were made; then the salt water in front of them parted, revealing the track to the Holy Island guiding a safe way through the quicksands.

The whole party were able to walk to Lindisfarne with dry feet, carrying the sacred remains of their saint. The waters closed again behind them, preventing any others from following.

SNAKES AND AMMONITES

Here's a lovely little story that gives an explanation for the fossils found along the Whitby coast. St Hilda (AD 614–680) was an important and powerful figure in the early Church of Anglo-Saxon England. The monk Bede, who was born about eight years before Hilda died, noted: 'All who knew her called her mother because of her outstanding devotion and grace.'

The bells of Whitby Abbey were said to have been taken on a ship to London in 1539 after the abbey was dissolved by Henry VIII. However, local folklore says that the ship refused to carry the bells away, preferring to sink in the bay within sight of the abbey ruins. The bells, apparently, ring underwater to this day.

Ammonites are the fossilised shells of prehistoric creatures, one of the many fossil types found around the coasts of Britain. Due to their coiled shape, ammonites are also known as 'snakestones'. Another little folk tale says that St Keynes in Somerset changed snakes into rocks through her prayers.

In the year AD 655, when Oswy the king of Northumbria was at war with the heathen Mercians and their leader Penda, there was a great battle. Before he strapped on his battle gear and went to face the danger, Oswy vowed that if he were to see victory that day, he would give his tiny daughter Ethelfleda to a monastic life in thanks to God, and he would found twelve religious houses on his estates.

Oswy won the battle. The infant princess was given over to a nun called Hilda, who was also charged with being the first abbess at his new abbey in Whitby.

But the new abbey had problems. Almost immediately, the place was plagued by serpents and snakes, writhing over the ground, down the walls and out of the very stones that made the buildings. Hilda prayed, and encouraged all the others of holy orders to pray, that the snakes would go into the sea and never return.

Hilda was a practical woman, and she didn't just rely on prayer. After a long session of communion with God, she took up her whip and attacked the writhing creatures, slicing off their heads and tails and leaving their bodies coiled up on the floor. In horror, the creatures became petrified and turned to stone, and so they were easily cleared from the abbey and into the sea.

Even today, you might find the remains of one of St Hilda's snakes washed up on the sands at Whitby, and now you know their story.

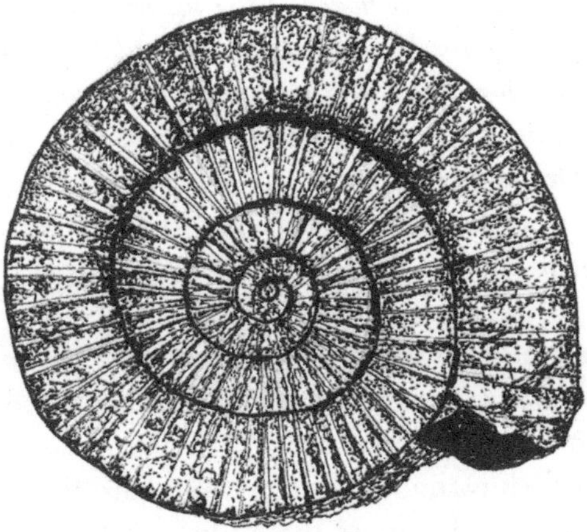

Chips

Many of our folk tales were told from memory to collectors of stories when they were children. This torrid tale was told to a certain Charles Dickens by his nurse Mary Weller, before he was 6 years old. Dickens later noted, in 1860's The Uncommercial Traveller, *that 'her name was Mercy, though she had none on me,' and remarked on the vivid and sometimes harrowing scenes recalled from the stories told to him as a child. Mary Weller's tales clearly had a lasting effect on Dickens' imagination – it's an example of the power of the oral storytelling tradition.*

This story, derived from Dickens' 1861 memoir, is unusual. Instead of doing a deal with the Devil of his own accord, Chips has inherited a family expectation that a deal with the Devil must be struck, as it was with his ancestors. Chips junior tries to bargain just the same, but it is the Devil's furry accomplice who has the last laugh.

Here is one of many stories speaking from the heart about the horror of rats on ships.

Young Chips never wanted any trouble. He had learned that trouble was a Bad Thing, no matter how it was dressed up, and he was determined to have a quiet life.

Chips was a shipwright and he worked hard in a government yard. His father had worked there too, and he was also called Chips, and his father before him had worked in the same place, although the ships were different then, and his name was Chips too. There was a whole long line of Chipses, with their work and toil and craft sailing the high seas of goodness-knows-where. But this Chips, the hero of our story, stayed safely in the yard.

For young Chips had a dark secret. The truth was that his father, Chips senior, had sold his soul to the Devil, and what for? Nothing but an iron pot, a bushel of tenpenny nails, half a ton of copper and a rat that could speak: all of these could be very useful things for a shipwright.

But it wasn't just his father. Chips's grandfather had also sold his soul for exactly the same: an iron pot, a bushel of tenpenny nails, half a ton of copper and a rat that could speak. Chips's great grandfather had also done the same bargain with Old Nick, and his father before him. So his legacy went back and back. Chips bemoaned his forefathers' lack of imagination, and their lack of backbone.

'I won't have it,' said Chips. 'There's no reason why I should be the same as them. I will be a fine, upstanding member of the community, me. I don't want any trouble. A nice quiet life for me.'

But sometimes our fate is stronger than our desire.

One day, when young Chips was hammering down in the dark hold of an old ship hauled up for repairing, he felt someone was watching, so he paused his hammer and looked up. There on the stair, slouching against a pile of old wood, was the Devil, with a crooked grin, and silver buttons on his coat.

The Devil looked at young Chips and it seemed that his red eyes bored into the young lad's soul. He remarked, 'A lemon has pips, and a yard has ships, and I'll have Chips!'

The Devil gurned and winked at Chips. Blue sparks flew out from under his eyelids, as if tiny flints had been struck on them. Chips could see that hanging over the Devil's arm like a handbag was the handle of a smart iron pot, and at his feet was a bushel of tenpenny nails, and what looked like half a ton of copper.

But more than all of that – dancing on the shoulder of the Devil was a small brown furry creature, with its bald fleshy tail twitching in the air, its pale nose sniffing for trouble, and its beady black eyes darker than the pits of Hell itself.

Chips tried to look away and he tried to run, but his feet were rooted to the spot. The Devil brought his head round and made him meet the infernal eyes, and he said again, 'A lemon has pips, and a yard has ships, and I'LL HAVE CHIPS!'

Chips decided it was best not to answer at all. He picked up his hammer and carried on working.

'What are you doing, Chips?' asked the rat in a high, squeaky voice.

'I'm putting in new planks, where the old planks have been eaten away by your brothers and sisters,' said Chips.

'Ah, Chips,' said the rat, 'that's wasted work, honestly, because we'll eat those planks too. We'll let in the water and the crew will drown, and then we will eat the crew too, and we'll have a huge party.'

'Doesn't matter to me,' said Chips. 'I'm only a shipwright, I don't sail in the bloody things.'

But his eyes wandered to the bushel of tenpenny nails and the half a ton of copper on the floor of the hold.

The rat squealed with laughter and the Devil roared, 'I saw you, Chips! You can't help yourself. Why don't you strike the bargain? You know the terms. They are the same terms I struck with your father, and your grandfather and great grandfather. It doesn't matter where they are now … but they did well when they were alive, as well you know.'

Chips took a deep breath, and then wished he hadn't, because it was full of sulphur.

'See here, your … Devilship,' coughed Chips. 'I'm not my father, or my father's father. The copper and the nails, they are fine enough for a shipwright to have, and the iron pot is decent enough – but I don't like the rat, and I won't have him, on any account.'

The rat stopped dancing and just stared, wringing his tiny paws together, although Chips couldn't tell whether it was gleeful or glum.

The Devil's red eyes flashed. 'You can't dictate your own terms here, Chips. If you don't have the rat, you can't have any of the rest of it. I'm going.'

'Hold on!' cried Chips, suddenly worried about losing all the metal he'd been offered. 'Give those here!'

The Devil disappeared then, in a puff of foul-smelling smoke. Chips looked down, and on the floor was the bushel of tenpenny nails, the iron pot, and the half a ton of copper.

Sitting on his shoulder, flicking its tail against his neck in victory, was the rat.

It looked like the deal had been struck, although Chips wasn't entirely sure.

Chips sold the bushel of tenpenny nails and the half a ton of copper. He went to sell the pot too, but every time he looked inside, there was the rat jumping up and down and squeaking insults at him, and it wasn't a good look for potential buyers.

So Chips decided to kill the rat, and he thought long and hard about how to do it. One day on deck of a ship, Chips found the perfect opportunity, with the pot (and rat inside) on one side of him and a giant pot of scalding-hot pitch on the other.

Quick as a flash, Chips poured the scalding-hot pitch on top of the rat and filled the iron pot full. As the pitch cooled it hardened, and he left the pot alone for a couple of weeks. After that, just to be sure, he asked the smelters in the shipyard to put the pot and the pitch in the smelter for three full weeks more. After the three weeks were up, they brought out the pot for Chips, red-hot, and put it on the ground …

There was the rat, dancing up and down inside the pot, laughing at him! Chips supposed it had dealt with hotter things in the furnaces of Hell. The rat caught Chips's eye with its beady black eyes and squeaked with all its might, 'A lemon has pips, and a yard has ships, And I'LL HAVE CHIPS!'

'Typical,' thought Chips, 'this creature will be sticking to me from now on.'

'I will indeed,' squeaked the rat, as if it could read his mind. 'I'll stick to you like pitch. Ha – see what I did there?' It jumped out of the pot and ran off, and this gave Chips a tiny little bit of hope that it wouldn't do as it said.

The next day, Chips worked hard all day in the shipyard and he hoped he'd seen the last of the wretched rat. The bell struck for the end of work and Chips went up for dinner, reaching in his trouser pocket for his pocket handkerchief.

But there was no handkerchief in his pocket. There was a rat. An ordinary rat, but a rat nonetheless. Under his hat, there was another rat, and in his coat sleeves, there were two more rats. Chips's body was overrun with the tiny pink feet of rats, the slithering tails of rats, the brown fur, the chunky rodent bodies, the tiny sharp teeth, and – worst of all – the whiskers.

From that day onwards, from the time of waking to when he tried to grab a wink of sleep, Chips's life was wretched with rats. They would sit around and observe his work, climb up his trouser legs, wave from his teapot, hide in his tool bag, nibble the laces on his boots, sip at his jug of beer. That wasn't the strangest of it. Although these rats didn't speak, Chips could understand their squeaking, and they could understand him. It was almost as if Chips was now considered part of their lives and dialogue. He had become an honorary rat.

Now Chips had been betrothed all this time to a fine young lass, although he had taken care to keep any mention of rats and devils as far away from her as he could. He had worked on a wooden box that he had lovingly made just for her, and the day came to present her with the gift, but when she opened it, a big fat rat jumped out of it. Naturally, she screamed, but when he put his arm around her shoulders to comfort her, another rat ran straight down her spine.

So Chips found himself without a sweetheart because of all the rats, and when the banns were called off in the church and the vicar got out the register, a large brown rat scurried over the page and over his hand.

Poor Chips. Now his whole life was about rats, and somehow with a kind of rat-knowing he could see in his head what all the rats were doing, even if he couldn't see them with his eyes. Rats being rats, this was not very pleasant, and sometimes he would call out, 'Oh! That's horrible! Someone chase the rats out of the graveyard before they do that again!'

Or, 'They're eating all the butter in the stores!'

Or, 'Mind you get the shipyard-master to go home, there's two of them sniffing at the baby in the crib!'

And so on.

At last, Chips lost his job, because he was declared by the others at the shipyard to be quite mad. It was difficult to get another job, and he needed to eat. Then he found out that the king needed sailors, and he signed up.

That's how Chips found himself taken off in a small boat towards a great ship that was destined to sail to the Indies. As he looked up at the creaking old vessel, he recognised it: the very same old ship he had been working on in the shipyard when he saw the Devil! Her name, *Argonaut*, was painted on the side as they rowed under the bowsprit with its figurehead.

Dancing on its hind legs on top of the figurehead was a large brown rat.

'Chips!' it squeaked. 'Chips, Chips my good fellow! We've done it! We've eaten all the new boards, almost eaten them through. Once we've done that, we'll drown all the crew, and then we'll eat them too!'

That night, Chips felt a pit of dread in his belly as he lay in the hold and felt the ship lurch away from its moorings. They sailed, and sailed, and sailed, and Chips could not bring himself to look ahead to where they were going, for he knew only too well.

Finally, one day Chips asked to speak to the admiral, and he went down on his knees in the admiral's cabin. 'Your Honour, make haste, sail to the nearest shore, or we are doomed and all will be lost! They are nibbling us to death.'

'Young man, you rave like a madman,' said the admiral. 'Who are "they" that you refer to?'

'Them rats, Your Honour, and that's the truth. The hull of this ship is not solid oak, it's all been eaten through, and it's about to break! All those pointed teeth, all of them working to kill every one of us. If you ever want to see your loved ones again, Your Honour, make for the shore!'

'My poor fellow,' said the admiral, 'you are not a well man. Fetch the doctor!'

So Chips had all manner of nasty treatments that passed for medicine, bitter herbs and bleeding and cold baths, all the time watching rats running along the ship's timbers and laughing at him in their high squeaky voices.

After six days, Chips struggled free from his leg bindings and ran to the admiral's cabin again, where he cried out, 'Now, Your Honour, we will all die, and you along with us! I warned you, but you wouldn't listen! The rats tell me they will have eaten through everything at midnight tonight, and the rats are never wrong. Nothing we can do now will stop them.'

Chips was carried away, kicking and screaming, and tied up for his own safety.

At midnight that night, there was a groaning of timbers and a rushing of seawater, and a great hole opened up in the hull of the ship, right where Chips had been mending it. Nothing could stop the water pouring in, and the ship went down into the cold salt ocean, with all souls on board, including Chips.

The rats survived, though. They made short work of the wreckage and long feasting of the ship's contents.

What the rats left of poor Chips, still bound with rope, floated eventually towards the shore in a mass of seaweed. Standing on top of that mass danced a large brown rat, laughing and laughing, with its bald fleshy tail twitching in the air, its pale nose sniffing for trouble, and its beady black eyes darker than the pits of Hell itself. As soon as the remains touched the shore, the rat dived into the sea and was never seen again … or was it?

If you gathered thirteen bits of that seaweed, and dried them in the air, and then burned them, they would whine and squeal and make the flames go blue, and if you listened carefully you would hear the words: 'A lemon has pips, and a yard has ships, and I'VE GOT CHIPS!'

THE PARSON AND THE CLERK

Dawlish is a Devon seaside resort close to the point where the Exe estuary meets the sea, near to Teignmouth. It was little more than a fishing village until the beginning of the nineteenth century. Brunel's railway line, constantly mended and upgraded, still runs along the coast here in defiance of both engineers and storms. Dawlish is also famous for its black swans. It's the home of the famous Devon Violets perfume that I remember from my grandmother's dressing table when I was little.

The Parson and the Clerk are two rocks that can be seen clearly from the railway line and the South-West Coast Path near Dawlish. The Parson leans against the headland, while the Clerk is a little way out into the sea.

This story was first recorded by an anonymous author in 1848. They mused that when the main part of the Clerk rock was eroded in a storm in 1824, a large part of the suffering of the Clerk (the lesser sinner) must have been released, while the taller Parson's rock remained as 'a sad and disastrous monument of the effects of clerical cupidity'.

In their own versions, Edwin Hartland in 1906 and Robert Hunt in 1908 included the story in their collections on the basis that 'seeing that this forms a part of Old Cornwall, I do not go beyond my limits in telling the true story of these singular rocks'. I think most Devonians would take issue with that!

A 'blackjack' is a leather drinking vessel or tankard, sealed with tar on the inside.

The Bishop of Exeter was gravely ill at Dawlish. Some whispered that he might not recover, although they had been whispering that for years. Many people visited the holy man to help bring some cheer and companionship.

A particular parson appeared in Devon at that time from another diocese. Nobody knew it, but this man's soul thirsted for a higher office in the Church, and God had not seen fit to award it yet. He had heard that the Bishop of Exeter had a wasting disease and was not long for this world. So he began to visit the bishop at his summer residence in Dawlish very often, riding from east Devon on his black mare to enquire after the condition of his Grace. This parson was a little too eager, a little too keen, as a man might be keen if he was only interested in gaining the role of bishop after the present incumbent had vacated it.

The parson's clerk was a faithful man and usually rode his little grey nag alongside his master's horse, as he knew the roads well and could guide him. But on one particular rough and stormy night, they lost the road just after the estuary. Both parson and clerk found themselves wandering over Haldon Hill, which was a most unsavoury place, full of trees and shadows.

The parson was angry, and the clerk was anxious, and he kept trying this road and that direction and all manner of ways forward. Yet they could not find the right road, and at one point had definitely gone round in a circle. The rain was pelting down now, and they were both soaked through.

Finally, they reached a point where the track went in no fewer than five different directions. The parson, exasperated, cried out, 'For Heaven's sake! I would rather have the Devil himself for a guide, than you!'

They pressed on. Presently, there was a scuffle and a clatter of hooves on the stones, and there was a smelly old peasant on his little moorland pony, out in the rain on his own.

'Hey! You, fellow! Can you guide me to Dawlish better than this idiot of a companion of mine?' called the parson.

'I be a'goin' to Dawlish meself,' came the reply. 'Follow me.'

They rode on through driving rain, scarcely able to make out the road more than a few paces ahead of them, but the track travelled downwards and roundaboutwards as if it was going somewhere. It felt like an age, and the sound of the sea grew louder as they rode, sometimes so loud that both the parson and the clerk feared that they would go over the edge into the water. Eventually, they found themselves riding into Dawlish, just as the rain was abating and the biting cold properly found them all.

'I 'bide een 'in,' said the peasant, 'there's grub an' a change o' clothes, if ye don' mind a bit of earthiness.'

The parson was ravenous after the long journey, and soaked to the bone. If he had thought about it, he would have realised the clerk was too. They rode towards an old stone house, surprisingly large for such a peasant, with bright lights flickering through the filthy windows. It was a hearth, and that was welcome enough on such a night.

The peasant's kitchen was full of people, all gathered together around a rickety old table, and a wild-looking lot they were. But the table was groaning with food, and covered with blackjacks, and to both the parson and the clerk this looked very agreeable. They joined the merry company, and soon there were smiles, and toasts, and nods of agreement.

Time rolled by in an entertaining fashion, and the drink flowed, first the cider, and then the brandy and rum. Within an hour or so, the parson was telling stories about the strangest of his parishioners, and the oddest of odd confidences. In no time at all, he was dancing on the flagstone floor and singing hunting songs.

Then with a loud belch, a pat of his belly and a roll of his eyes to the heavens, the parson began to sing one very particular hunting song, a hunting song they all knew, about a certain Old Nick, with whom no priest should ever admit any acquaintance. The men round the table roared their approval at this irreverence, and all of them knew the choruses to sing, with the filthiest of words.

So the night went on, until in the small hours there was a rap at the door and a traveller appeared, ashen-faced, out of the night and into the kitchen.

'His Grace the Bishop is dead,' he stammered.

The parson was standing on the kitchen table at the time, with a tankard of cider in his hand. 'So let's raise a toast to the miserable old sinner, then, shall we? I'll do a much finer job, won't I lads?' There were more laughs and shouts of approval as the parson jumped from the table and walked out into the night to find his horse, followed by the clerk who was holding on to the table for dear life as he went.

So, there they were, the parson sitting on his black mare and the clerk sitting on his little grey nag, both holding on much too tightly to the reins and the saddles to keep their balance. But the horses refused to move.

'Confound it! The Devil himself is in these horses!' cried the parson.

'D' you know, I believe he really is,' said the clerk.

'Devil or no Devil, they – will – MOVE!' shouted the parson, whipping his poor horse.

But the horse would still not budge, and now they were surrounded by an unearthly laughter, coming up from the ground itself.

The drinking fellows all surrounded the parson and the clerk on their horses. Their faces looked up, and their hands grasped at the feet of the two men, and their mouths cackled. They were no longer in human form, but demons. Up strode their guide – the old peasant man. He threw his hood away from his face, chuckling with manic glee, sharp teeth and a deep red twinkle in his eyes.

Although they were a little way from the shore, the noise of the waves was loud now. The parson turned wildly towards the house, but it had gone. The waves were already crashing against the flanks of his horse, and they had all but submerged both the clerk and his pony.

He was surrounded now, not by demons, but by the dark, cold salt water, relentlessly beating him and then receding, each time carrying a little more of his soul away. It was much too late to repent.

The following morning, two lone horses were found wandering the sands at Dawlish. The parson's body was suspended from the large stone propped against the cliff, while the clerk was facing seaward, clinging to a rock in the sea in mortis.

They gave their names to the rocks that remain at Dawlish to this day.

3

FISHING FOR FORTUNE

Dance to thy daddy, sing ti' thy mammy,
Dance to thy daddy, ti' thy mammy sing,
Thou shalt have a fishy on a little dishy,
Thou shalt have a bloater when the boat comes in.

Traditional English folk song

Since the first people came here, there have probably been people fishing from the sea. A huge array of different fish species live in the waters around England's coasts, invisible to most of the population until they end up on our dinner plates.

England's important fishing ports hold many stories, from Brixham in Devon to Grimsby, once the largest fishing port in the world. Our sea-fishing industry has developed over the centuries from humble efforts supported by whole communities, through to international trade and foreign markets, to the modern industrial scallop dredgers that decimate life across the seabed. In 2022, UK vessels landed 640,000 tonnes of sea fish with a value of £1.04 billion.

Sadly, as with the land, the millions of species in the seas around England have suffered as our capability to harvest them has become more efficient and industrial. The Marine Conservation

Society estimates that globally, over 90 per cent of world fish stocks are fully or over-exploited from fishing. Small as well as large fish are taken, to the point where there are not enough left to regenerate healthy fish populations. UK herring and cod populations crashed in the 1970s and despite a partial recovery of both, cod stocks are again below safe biological levels.

The over-exploitation of sea fish has led to significant change in the English fishing industry. It makes sense to fish at levels that are sustainable for the long term. Efforts to stop over-fishing include setting fishing quotas and identifying marine protected areas to help fish populations and their ecosystems recover – an approach which has met with success in some cases around English coasts. Yet Charles Clover noted in 2022 that 97 per cent of our protected marine areas in the UK are still fished in some way – most are trawled – and that the area of England's coastal waters that is fully protected from any intervention covers a smaller area than the City of Westminster. The war between short-term gain and long-term sustainability is a depressingly familiar story that continues ever on.

In the meantime, fish and chips is still an English national dish, and sea fish remain an important part of our culture. We can all help by keeping up to date with the Good Fish Guide, actively choosing the fish we eat, and buying it from more sustainably fished sources. The excellent Marine Conservation Society and Marine Stewardship Council websites both have plenty more information.

Here's a selection of English folk tales about fish and fishing to whet your appetite.

The Fairest of All Others

This story is about the sea deciding the fate of people. It has many versions all over England. This one was collected by T.W. Thompson from Tammi Boswell, a Roma storyteller, in early twentieth-century Yorkshire.

What is 'fair'? Beautiful women in traditional tales are often not considered any more than skin deep and, by the standards of any time, they are frequently treated poorly. My version of this story challenges some of the old tropes, and asks some questions that the characters may not want to answer.

There was a poor fisherman and his wife, and they lived in the same little house at the coast they had lived in all their lives. They had never been blessed with children, but they had come to terms with that long ago, and now they were much older they lived as best as they could with all the village folk helping each other.

One day, the fisherman was heading out towards his boat when he heard a little mewling cry from the rocks. He walked over to investigate, and there was something strange floating about in one of the bigger rock pools near to the shore. As he got closer, he could see a little box made of pale-coloured wood, all soaked in the salt water, but floating.

When he got to the box he gasped. There inside, all wrapped up in a blanket and dry as can be, was a little baby girl, her face screwed up and wailing. She wasn't a newborn, but she wasn't very old either. Of course, he got the infant out of that box and wrapped her in woollens as soon as he could, and then he walked back up the beach and took the little one, still crying, back to his wife in the cottage.

When the little one had calmed down, she opened her eyes to look around and everyone was dazzled by her piercing green eyes. The fisherman and his wife were, naturally, enchanted by this beautiful child that had come to them so late in life.

'But we are so old now!' said the fisherman's wife. 'We can bring her up well for as long as we live, but where will she go then?'

The story spread through the village about the little child found in the sea, and nobody came forward to claim her. But a lot of people came to look at her, and wonder about where she came from. Was she a mermaid's child, with those eyes of the sea?

Among them was the young squire's son from the nearby estate. He considered himself to be a worldly fellow, although he was all of 18 years old. They said he spoke several languages and was well versed in science and art. Some even said he was interested in magic.

The squire's son ducked under the door lintel of the little cottage to see the child. In the corner, several others crowded round the simple crib.

'Poor little mite,' said the squire's son, looking with distaste at the humble room around him, and peering into the cradle. 'I wonder what future she'll have.'

An old woman turned around, seeing her chance. 'I can tell you that, m' lord. For a fee I will tell her fortune. Five pieces of silver.'

The impertinence of it! Everyone looked to the squire's son and waited for a reply.

'Very … well, let's hear it,' he said, curious, and took out his purse.

'I'll go to get my cards,' she said.

He followed her outside, despite himself. It wasn't long before he was sitting in an even more decrepit hovel, with the woman's filthy hand grasping his own and peering at his palm. She consulted her cards again, threw some pebbles on the table, and finally sat back, threw her head back and cackled.

'What's so funny?' he said, 'I won't be laughed at by a peasant. I shall leave now, and take my money back!'

'Nay, nay, stay a while and listen,' she said. 'The signs are as clear as anything. That little girl will marry a grand fellow one day. All the oracles are telling me the same thing: the grand fellow she marries, sir, it will be you. That little girl is your fate, and if you try to deny her, it will be the worse for you.'

The cackles followed him as the squire's son stormed out. He strode down on the beach to think about what he had been told. This could not be. This WOULD not be. Marrying a peasant girl fished from the sea? What did the fortune-teller know?

He decided on a course of action.

First, he went back to the hovel of the fortune-teller and paid her to keep quiet, on pain of death, or at least being hounded out of the village.

Then he went back to the fisherman's hut. There were the fisherman and his wife with the child, all other visitors gone.

This time he was polite: he knocked on the door before he came in; he walked in and pulled up a chair.

'What is it?' said the fisherman's wife? 'What portents has she seen?'

'Oh, there's nothing to worry about,' said the squire's son. 'This little girl has a rich and unusual life ahead of her, of that there's no doubt. But she will need better circumstances to make the most of her life. I have thought the matter over and I am prepared to adopt the child, if you will allow me. I will pay you good money for the privilege.'

With that the squire's son brought out a bag of gold and put it on the rickety old cottage table. 'Think it over,' he said. 'I'll be back in the morning.'

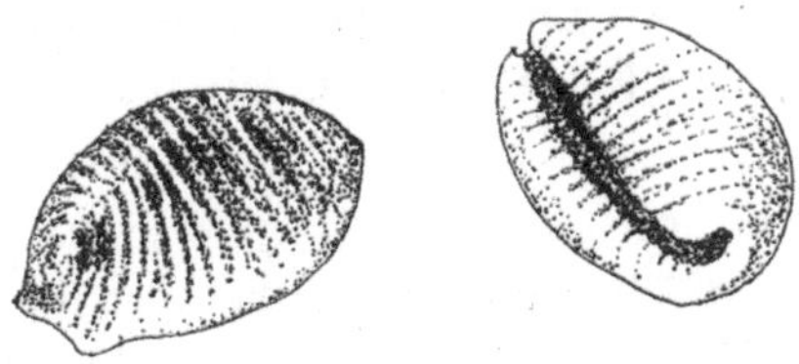

That night the fisherman and his wife talked and talked.

'That fine household would give her the best chance in life,' said the fisherman.

'But we've never been blessed with a child, and now the chance comes along we can't throw it away!' cried his wife.

The following day, they had decided. 'It's for her own welfare,' said the fisherman, handing over the child all wrapped in the woollen blanket. 'Take care of her.'

'I will,' said the squire's son, and rode away with the precious bundle.

He rode for a good hour, all across the peninsula to the coast on the other side. As they approached the sea, the baby started to wail.

'I'll give you something to cry about,' said the squire's son. He grabbed an old wooden fishing crate from outside one of the fishing huts and put the baby inside it. Then his horse picked its way across the rocks around towards the headland and out of sight of people, and he threw the box and the baby into the sea.

Later that afternoon, a fisherman on a boat coming back into shore spotted an old box bobbing up and down in the waves. He pulled it in, and was astonished to find a baby girl inside, dehydrated and poorly.

'There's a fine catch for you,' joked his friends. 'Seems this coast is full of babies, so why not one for you and your wife?'

Back onshore, he hurried home with the little girl, and his wife managed to revive the baby with some warm milk.

'We've already got four little ones,' said his wife, 'a fifth would be perfect.'

They called the little girl Betsy. She grew up to be a fine, strong girl, inside and out. Whenever any issue between the village children needed to be solved, or an argument settled, they always called on Betsy, because she was the fairest-minded child in the whole village.

When Betsy was 17 years old, she was serving ale in the local tavern when two men she didn't recognise came in to the bar. They were both smartly dressed, clearly both squires, men of means.

'You're a fine-looking maid,' said one.

'Yes, look at the green of her eyes! Sometimes peasant girls can be beauties!' laughed the other. Betsy looked down and blushed.

'Let's see.' The first squire was unnerving her now. He held her chin in his hand and forced her to look at him. 'Those eyes are … quite something, yes. Now tell me my dear, which family do you come from in this wretched village?'

'I … don't … know, sir,' she stammered. 'Me dad found me in the sea, so they say.'

The first man was paler now. 'How interesting!' quipped the second. 'Maybe there are mermaids after all, eh!'

It was several days later when the first squire from the tavern came riding by Betsy's house, just as she was bringing two pails of water back from the village pump.

'Hello again my dear! Is this your house?'

'Yes … Yes, sir,' she stammered.

He rapped on the door and Betsy's father answered. Inside, they came to a deal. The squire man wanted a cook for his household, and Betsy would do a fine job. There'd be a good wage in it.

Betsy had no say in the matter. She was whisked away on the man's horse and her father was left looking stunned with a large bag of gold in his hand.

The squire's son – for it was he – rode with Betsy for one hour, then two hours, and then up on to the clifftop overlooking the great blue ocean, out through gorse and buckthorn, out to the very edge. There he stopped, and dragged Betsy off the horse into a patch of thorns.

'For the love of God,' he snarled. 'I thought I had got rid of you once; this time I will make sure of it!'

'I don't understand!' she cried. 'What have I ever done to hurt you? I'm only a poor fisherman's daughter, I've done you no harm at all!' Then she screamed at the flash of his sword, and prayed and pleaded to her maker that the end of her life should be quick.

She waited with eyes screwed tight, but there was a pause. Then he let her go and she fell back into the gorse. The bright green eyes opened. She was still alive.

He was taking a golden ring off his hand, with some difficulty, then he held it up to the light.

'See this?' His voice was strained. 'This is the ring of my mother, who died many years ago. When I began wearing it, I swore that no other woman would ever have a hold over me. No other woman!'

He threw the ring out into the wide blue sea.

'I never want to see you again. If I ever see you, and you do not carry the ring, I will kill you, I swear it. If you do find the ring, then perhaps the fates are at play, but you never will find it. How could you?'

He got back on his horse and rode away in haste, leaving Betsy a terrified heap on the ground, sobbing.

'I never want to see you again neither,' she said, wiping her face.

Then she walked.

Betsy couldn't go back home in case she saw the squire, and so she walked in the opposite direction, and she walked for several days, sleeping where she could in caves and in the woods.

Finally, after miles and miles, she came to a great house, knocked on the door and asked for work.

The house was owned by a grand lady who took an instant liking to Betsy and gave her a job in the kitchens. To her great credit, the grand lady didn't ask about Betsy's circumstance or background, and Betsy never told her.

Betsy worked hard, and soon her innate fairness and kindness shone through. Everyone liked Betsy. It wasn't too long before she became housekeeper for the great house. Although she was sad about never seeing her parents or family, the thought of that monster – and the harm she might come to – kept her away. She earned enough money to live well and happily, in a good community of people who worked at the house, and it was enough for her.

Years went by. One day a man came up to the house who was selling fish from the boats. Betsy bought several large fish for a feast that evening, and down in the kitchen she helped the cooks clean and gut the fish.

She took a knife to the belly of a great silver fish, cut it open from head to tail and opened it out … there in its stomach was a gleam of gold.

Betsy felt her own stomach turning as she took out the golden ring and washed it clean. Was it the same ring? She knew in her heart it was; that's how these things happened.

Still, she didn't have to ever *see* him. It was just a gold ring. A token, perhaps, of how she had survived.

She put it on her finger and carried on with her work. Everyone else in the house 'ooh'-ed and 'aah'-ed at Betsy's luck in finding gold. 'She's married a fish!' they said, and she smiled to herself. They didn't know the full story.

Several weeks later, there was a party at the big house. Carriage after carriage drew up full of elegantly dressed people. The food was exquisite and the wine flowed. All the servants came up to see the dancing.

Two men were laughing with one another, making some kind of bet, then one of them came over to Betsy. 'May I have this dance?'

This was embarrassing; she was being ridiculed. She curtsied and agreed without properly looking at him.

But halfway through the dance, out there in front of everyone, she saw a twist in his grin that she recognised. He saw a familiar gold ring on her finger, and then he saw those green eyes.

The dance seemed to last for an age, and she could not look at him. As soon as the music finished, she tried to make her excuses and go. 'No!' whispered the squire. 'I must speak to you.'

She couldn't struggle and she couldn't make a scene in front of all the assembled company, and so the two of them left the great hall and walked in the garden.

She tried to run, but he caught her by the arm. 'I … I owe you the greatest of apologies for my behaviour,' he said immediately. 'I was young, and headstrong, and foolish. I am only glad I can truly say sorry to you in person.'

Betsy was speechless. All she could think of to do was to take the golden ring from her finger and give it back to him. 'This is yours,' she said, 'not mine.'

'Keep it?' he pleaded.

They began to talk.

Whether they ever spoke again after that night, I will leave for you to decide.

Robin Hood Turns Fisherman

Robin Hood needs no introduction as one of England's mythical folk heroes – but doesn't he usually live in the forest? Not in this tall tale, where he decides to try his hand at making a living from the sea. Robin is clearly a fish out of water here (excuse the pun) until it comes to the familiar craft of battle.

This is one of the later Robin Hood stories, first recorded in 1631 and widely published as a popular broadside ballad across the two centuries following. It was considered rather infantile by Francis James Child, the great folksong collector (the story and song is Child Ballad 148). Nevertheless, it's great fun to play with as a folk tale.

Robin Hood's Bay is a village on the Yorkshire coast about 15 miles north of Scarborough. In the sixteenth century, it was a more important port than Whitby, and has long traditions of fishing and smuggling. Lionel Charlton noted in his 1779 History of Whitby *that this Robin Hood ballad gave the hero's name to the village, but there are records of Robin Hood's Bay from much earlier in 1324. Who knows how the village really got its name?*

Winter was coming in, and there was scarce money coming in to the coffers of the merry company in Sherwood Forest. Nobles weren't offering up as much gold under duress, and assaults on the Great North Road weren't turning up the usual goods. Robin Hood feared for the welfare of the local people as well as for his own band of outlaws. They couldn't live on wits alone.

One fine day, Robin was in Scarborough, and saw the fishing boats with their fine catches of fish and their broad smiles. 'These men earn more than any merchant. Perhaps I should turn my hand to fishing,' he thought.

So Robin took up lodgings in an old inn, and that evening he got chatting to the landlady.

'We haven't seen you round here before,' she offered, 'what is your name?'

'Simon,' said Robin. 'As simple and as cheerful as the day is long.'

'Ah,' she said, smiling, 'perhaps you take after our fine saint of fishermen, Simon Peter.'

'Perhaps I do,' said Robin. 'Do you know of any crews on fishing boats that I could join?'

'Why, I own a boat myself,' she said. 'You shall go out to sea with them tomorrow, and if there's any trouble they'll have to answer to me.'

So the following morning, Simon (that was Robin) took his place on the fishing boat, smiling broadly at everyone there.

They didn't smile back. 'What on earth is he wearing?' they muttered to one another. 'I'd wager he won't survive five minutes out on the high sea. Never been out to sea in his life.'

They pluck't up anchor, and away did sayle,
More of a day then two or three;
When others cast in their baited hooks,
The bare lines into the sea cast he.

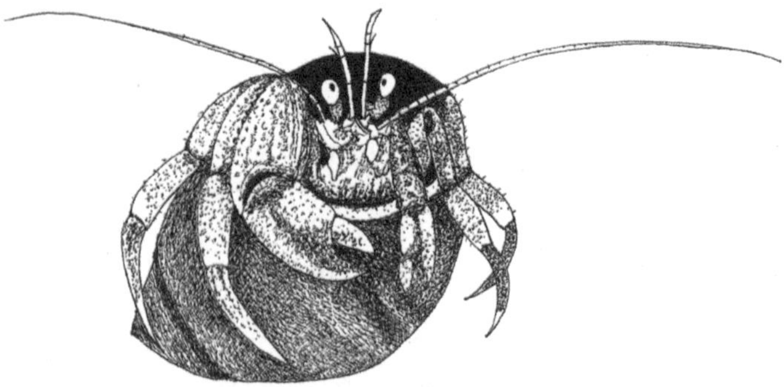

'Ha! Look what the land-lubber's doing!'

'You won't catch much in the way of fish without bait, love.'

'Waste of space, that idiot, why did he bother coming along?'

It's fair to say that fishing was not one of Robin's strong points, and nobody on the boat wanted to show him the ropes. Instead, the boat's master declared sternly, 'That Simon-lubber will have no part in the fish we bring back from this trip, for in truth, he has had no part in catching it.'

Robin gazed out to the rolling waves all around them, with no land in sight, and felt slightly queasy. 'I wish I were chasing deer in the great park,' he thought. 'Bet they couldn't do that.'

They pluck't up anchor, and away did sayle,
More of a day then two or three;
But Simon spied a ship of warre,
That sayld towards them most valourously.

'Woe is us!' said the Master. 'That's the enemy French, and now we will lose all the good fish we've caught. Look at them leering at us. We'll be thrown into their rotten prisons!'

'Don't worry about them,' announced Simon (that was Robin), 'I'll sort them out in no time.'

There was a silence, and nothing but the splash of waves and the creaking of timbers; then the whole boat erupted into laughter.

'Hark at 'im! He knows it all!'

'Let's hope he en't as bad at shooting as he is at fishing.'

'Will they take 'im as hostage? Then we can sail away and be rid of 'im.'

Robin said no more but took his bow and an arrow from the quiver on his back, drew the arrow back on the bow and let it fly. The arrow pierced the heart of one of the French sailors on deck, and he fell dead.

The others on the French ship shouted with alarm, but now Robin was following with more arrows, a volley of arrows, each one hitting its mark straight and true. The fishermen were agape. They could do little but watch, as every single one of the French sailors either died or scurried below deck.

It wasn't long before the fishermen were on board their captured French ship, the last of its original crew taken hostage and rendered helpless. Robin came up from below deck, grinning from ear to ear.

'I've counted about £12,000 in gold,' he said. 'How shall we divide it between us?'

The master of the fishing boat was now red-faced and shamed, cap in hand.

'Young Simon,' he said, 'we have been over-harsh on you, and I am ashamed to say it, as you saved our lives. We deserve little more than to live, and keep our fish, and keep our lives at your mercy.'

'Nay, nay,' laughed Simon (that was Robin). 'To keep you hostage is not my intention. I am content to live free and to help all the poor oppressed who suffer at the hands of tyranny, for my name is Robin Hood! Let's use this gold to good ends.'

So the fortune was used to help the poor people who lived in Robin Hood's Bay.

As for the fishing, Robin had his pride. He asked the fishermen, 'All I would ask, good sirs, is that you remember my skills with a bow and arrow, and forget my poor attempts at fishing. That is better left to the experts.'

But some of them clearly didn't do as Robin asked – for now this story has reached you.

The King of the Herrings

This is an old Roma tale, recorded in both England and Wales in the early twentieth century by folklore collectors T.W. Thompson and Dora Yates (I have worked elements of both versions into this one). It's a daft adventure of a fairy tale featuring our ubiquitous national anti-hero Jack. Some motifs in this story can be recognised in other tales: fish that promise to return a favour, and also the magical horse and feather, found in the famous Russian story of the Firebird.

*Atlantic or North Sea herring is the second most abundant fish in the world. Herring are related to other small forage fish species such as sardines and anchovies. Individual herring are typically about 8 inches long, but herring shoals can contain millions of fish and cover huge areas. Herring are an integral part of our marine food web, feeding on plankton and fish fry, and also forming a large part of the diet of gulls, gannets, dolphins, seals and most predatory fish including cod, bass and mackerel. Several other unrelated fish species, including giant oarfish (*Regalecus glesne*), are also nicknamed 'king of the herring' because of their great size.*

Once an important part of the nation's diet, Atlantic herring are traditionally smoked for kippers and bloaters, and pickled for roll-mops. In the second half of the twentieth century, kippers were almost as popular as cod in England, but since then they have declined in popularity as a foodstuff. It's a shame, because they are still relatively plentiful and cheap, and Marine Stewardship Council-certified herring is readily available at the time of writing.

There was a happy young lad who lived in a little house by the sea with his mother and father, and his name was Jack. He grew up, and eventually his father and mother died. Jack carried on living in the cottage, and worked, as his father had done, in the local quarry.

One day, on his day off, Jack was sitting outside his little cottage and watching the world go by, when an old man shuffled along past the front door.

'Hello! Nice day,' said Jack.

The old man fixed Jack with a beady eye.

'Perhaps it is, and perhaps it isn't. Will you adventure with me, so we can both seek our living?'

'All right,' said Jack. 'I'll do that.'

'Then here is what you have to do. Say you want to turn me into an old nag,' said the old man.

'I want to turn you into an old nag,' said Jack.

The old man disappeared and in his place was an old, tired horse, panniers across his back, with a shaggy mane and the same black beady eyes.

Jack jumped on the old horse's back and off they went.

'You must promise,' said the old nag as they rode away from the cottages and up the hill, 'if we find anyone in trouble on the way, you must be sure to find out what's the matter, and you must help if you can.'

'I promise,' said Jack.

They rode a long, long way, down the other side of the hill and down towards the coast road.

'I hear something calling out!' said Jack. The old nag trotted, then stopped. Jack got off its back and went down to the shore to investigate.

It was the herring time of autumn, and there, flapping on the sand and the gravel, was a little silver fish, stranded from the rest and gasping. Jack picked it up and put it back into the water.

The little herring swam as close to Jack's toes as it could, and poked its little silvery fish face out of the water. 'When you need me,' said the fish, 'call on me – the King of the Herrings – and I'll be there to help.'

'Thank you, I will,' Jack got back on the old nag and they were away.

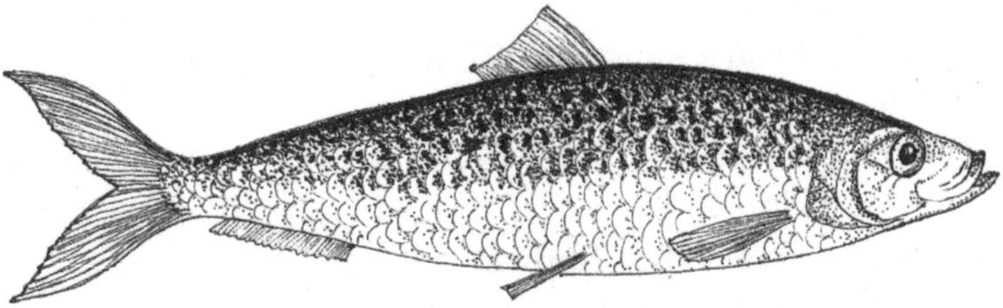

'You must promise,' said the old nag as they rode along, 'touch nothing that you see now, even if it is the finest thing that you have ever seen in your life.'

'I promise,' said Jack.

The wind blew a feather into Jack's mouth. He spluttered and took it out of his mouth. It blew back in. He took it back out and threw it back into the air. A third time the feather determinedly flew into Jack's mouth, and he took it out again and looked at it, gleaming green and gold in the sunlight.

'You're a pretty thing,' said Jack, 'you're coming with me,' and he put it in his pocket.

Now they came to an old castle, with a terrible loud sobbing coming from the inside. 'Go and see what the matter is, and I'll wait here,' said the nag. Jack went up and knocked on the gate; nobody answered, so he went in.

There was a giant lying on a bed, and he was very poorly – so ill he could do nothing for himself. His eyes were red from crying.

'What's the matter, friend?' said Jack.

'I've got nobody here to help me,' said the giant, 'nobody to get me food or drink. Could you go and get me a plate of food and a tankard of ale from the cellar?'

Jack did just that, and after the giant had eaten and drunk his fill, he began to feel a little better. 'If ever you need me,' said the giant, 'call on me, and I'll be there.'

'Thank you.' Now Jack was back on the old nag and they were riding fast downhill.

'What did you see on the hill back there, before the castle?' asked the nag.

'Nothing,' said Jack, 'only a green and gold feather than blew into my mouth.'

'Did you – take – the – feather?'

'Yes, it's here in my pocket as a matter of fact.'

The old nag groaned. 'That will bring us misfortune, but now you have it, keep it, do not let it go.'

Next they came to a mansion and Jack knocked on the door looking for work. He was taken into the kitchens to help with the pots and the cleaning. Jack had work; all was good.

But the very next day Jack knocked over a valuable vase and it smashed on the floor.

The master of the house was an affected fellow, all airs and graces and lace. He was vexed at the broken vase. 'Jack,' he said, 'Jack, that vase was worth its weight in gold. Do you have any money that can pay for the breakage?'

'None at all,' said Jack, 'nothing but this feather in my pocket, here.'

The whole household marvelled at the green and gold feather. 'This is a wondrous thing,' said the master. 'It will more than pay for the vase.'

The servants were jealous of Jack, and in the coming days they whispered in the master's ear, 'If he can get the feather, he can get the whole bird!' The master thought this was a wonderful idea.

Jack went to find the old nag. 'The master has ordered me to get the whole bird,' said Jack to the old nag. 'Very well,' said the nag, 'tell him you will need three days and three purses of gold.'

Weighed down with gold, they set off down the road, and it wasn't long before they came to another castle. 'Go in,' said the nag, 'and you will find a room full of people sitting at table, feasting. Touch nothing. In the corner there will be a sorry-looking bird in a cage, and its tail will be made of feathers like the one you gave to the master. Go and take it, but don't hang about.'

Jack got the bird and they took it back to the master. He had the poor thing put safely in a bigger, gilded cage, where it looked slightly less bedraggled but still pretty sorry for itself. The cage was hung up in the window and the sunlight and the light glittered off the bird's green and gold tail feathers.

The master looked at it wistfully. 'If only it was as easy to find my own true love as it was to get this bird with the splendid feathers!'

The servants were jealous of Jack, and in the coming days they whispered in the master's ear, 'If he can get the bird, he can get your true love as well!' The master thought this was a wonderful idea.

Jack went to find the old nag. "The master has ordered me to get his true love,' said Jack to the old nag.

'I did warn you about the feather, to be fair,' said the old nag, 'but it can't be helped. Go and ask him for three more days and three bags of gold. Bags of gold, mind, not purses.'

They were off on the road again then, chatting as they went, back down to the coast. The old nag said, 'Jack, make a wish that I become a ship on the sea.'

So Jack made the wish, and instantly there was a stately wooden galleon on the ocean, its great sails unfurled; and there was Jack, standing on board. The ship was laden with silks and finery of all colours.

The ship sped ahead, out to the blue ocean, the waves glittering and glimmering in the sunlight. On the other side of the wide bay there were rocks, and on the rocks was a castle. They sailed right up beneath the rocks on which the castle was built.

The ship's masts creaked. 'Jack, go up to the castle and ask to see the lady of the place. It's not the woman who greets you, by the way.'

Jack put boards out to the rocks and went to the gate of the castle. A young housekeeper opened it. 'I want to see the lady of this castle,' said Jack.

Out came the great lady. 'I have many silks on my ship,' said Jack, 'are you interested in buying them?'

It wasn't long before the lady of the castle was stepping with dainty feet on to the ship, and one of the crew led her to the cabin where the silks were stored. She gasped at the bright jewel colours of the cloth.

Jack stayed on deck, weighed anchor, and the ship sailed away.

Out in the deep ocean, the lady came out on deck and discovered that she had been tricked. She reached into her pocket and pulled out a great bunch of iron keys. With great drama, she flung them into the sea. At once, the sea turned crimson red like blood, storm clouds gathered, and the wind whipped up.

The ship kept sailing through it all, came safely to harbour, and changed back into the nag. Jack and the nag finally got back to the mansion with a very angry lady. Seeing the master didn't make her one bit happier. The master looked slightly scared of the lady, and wasn't quite sure what to do next.

One of the servants coughed to get the master's attention, and whispered in his ear, 'Whoever can get your own true love, he can also get the castle for you.'

Those servants really didn't like Jack.

Jack went to find the old nag. "The master has ordered me to get the castle as well,' said Jack to the old nag. 'How on earth can we do that?'

'I did warn you about the feather,' said the old nag, 'but it can't be helped. Go on, and ask him for three more days and three sacks of gold. Sacks of gold, mind, not bags.'

So they were away on the open road again, and riding fast. 'Let's go to the giant,' gasped the breathless old nag. 'Tell him what you want.'

Back at the giant's castle, the giant was feeling much better, and Jack found him playing a game of quoits in the woods, hurling huge rocks about the place.

'You want *what*?' chuckled the giant when Jack made his request. 'It'll need my biggest chain. Here!' The giant took Jack to an enormous iron chain lying on the ground. Jack couldn't lift a single link with all his strength, but the giant picked it up as if it were a piece of rope and slung it over his shoulder.

By the time Jack and the old nag had reached the lady's castle again, the giant had already waded through the sea and beaten them to it.

The giant put the huge chain around the lady's castle and its wall, and – heave! HEAVE! – dragged the castle on its rock, all the way through the water, to rest next to where the master's mansion overlooked the sea.

The master was delighted, the servants were jealous, but the lady was really not impressed. 'I can't even open the gate; it is locked,' she said. 'I'll need my keys.'

The old nag laughed. 'Jack, what was it the fish said?'

Jack knew immediately what he should do. He leapt on the old nag's back, and that poor old horse took Jack all along the coast road, all the way along the bay, until they reached the shore where Jack had originally stopped.

'King of the Herrings!' shouted Jack. 'King of the Herrings! I need your help! Please help!'

There was the little silvery fish face poking out of the sea. 'What is it, Jack?'

'I need the lady's bunch of iron keys – she threw them out in the ocean.'

'Wait there,' said the fish, 'I will find them.'

They waited. Jack and the nag waited, and waited, and waited some more, and still the King of the Herrings did not return.

'All is lost,' said Jack.

'Never doubt the King of the Herrings,' said the old nag.

Just as the sun touched the horizon in the west, there was the little fish at the shore again, exhausted.

'Where in the sea exactly are the keys?' asked the little herring. 'I've looked and looked everywhere and I can't see any keys.'

'I have no idea,' said Jack. 'Please, please find them though, it's really important!'

'I'll do my best for you Jack,' said the little fish, and it swam away again.

A whole day later, Jack was still looking out to sea and his eyes were going funny. But there – a flash of silver! It was a little silver fish with a big bunch of keys in mouth, five times as heavy as him.

'Thank you!' said Jack, and the King of the Herrings swam away into the deep blue ocean for a well-deserved rest.

Jack and the old nag returned to the castle. The gate was opened with the iron keys, and now all of them – master, lady, Jack and the old nag – were standing in the great parlour room of the castle.

'I won't thank you,' said the lady to Jack. 'Either you or the master must lose your head for what you have done. Tell me, Jack, you decide … Which of you is it to be?'

Jack looked at the old nag for advice. 'Choose carefully, Jack,' said the nag.

There was silence for a while. Jack shuffled his feet from side to side in deep thought, and then he spoke up.

'Since it was me that brought all of this trouble, I suppose it should be me who loses his head,' he said, and screwed his eyes up tight to wait for the blow to fall.

'You've answered well, Jack, you have answered very well,' said the lady. 'Had you given me a different answer, you would indeed have lost your head. But because you offered, it is your master who will go. He will not lose his head, but he will be banished to a faraway land.'

'I can help with that,' said the old nag. 'But first, Jack, don't forget your gold.'

There, in the panniers on the old nag, was all the gold the master had given them for their journeys. Jack was now a rich man, and the panniers on the back of the nag were empty again.

The master got on the back of the old nag, complaining and brushing the dirt from his fine clothes. They rode out to the coast road; they rode on, and on. Who knows where they got to? Perhaps they are still out there somewhere.

What about Jack?

Jack became the lord of that castle, and he married the lady, and they both lived happily ever after.

Stargazey Pie

Mousehole (pronounced 'Mouzle') is a pretty little Cornish fishing village about 2 miles south of Penzance. It's famous, among other things, for its Christmas illuminations, and a festival on 23 December – Tom Bawcock's Eve – celebrating the tale of this sixteenth-century local fisherman.

The story was apparently first recorded by Robert Morton Nance in 1927's Old Cornwall Journal, *together with a song he composed which has now become part of the local tradition:*

A merry plaace, you may believe,
Was Mouzel 'pon Tom Bawcock's Eve.
To be there then who wudn' wesh,
To sup o' sibm soorts o' fesh.
When morgy brath had cleared the path
Comed lances for a fry,
And then us had a bit o' scad,
An' starry-gazy pie!

Morton Nance questioned whether Tom Bawcock actually existed, although he seemed to think the festival itself had ancient origins. Other folklorists suggest that Stargazey Pie evolved from an older local ceremony, where fishermen baked fish into a pie that represented the variety of catch they wished for in the following year.

Mousehole was in trouble. It was coming up for Christmas and the storms had been terrible for weeks. Nobody had been able to go out on their boats, nor risk coming in to Mousehole with the huge waves. The villagers were starving hungry.

One fisherman, Tom Bawcock, decided to take matters into his own hands. One day just before Christmas he decided to venture out and get a catch somehow. He was a good sailor, and it was better to risk his life out there than sit around starving.

So, dodging the great waves, Tom took his little boat out of Mousehole harbour and into the swell. It was worse than he could have thought; between the gales and the breakers, it was all he could do just to keep the little vessel afloat.

Out went the lines and the hooks and the bait into the crashing water – if they would just stay attached! Tom stayed in that little boat just as long as he dared, the driving rain and the salt water trying to knock him over and swallow him up, and then he hauled and heaved the lines back in, calling for the fish to come and help him out.

Back to safety now. Tom managed to turn the boat around, eventually, and went back in, praying he wouldn't be dragged out to the rocks. One final wave pushed him into the little harbour and he was home. As the villagers ran to meet him with cheers and yells, a half-drowned Tom looked at the fishing lines; he'd caught plenty of fish for everyone to have a good old feast.

That night a great pie was made at the local inn, with seven different kinds of fish: pilchard, sand eel (lances), scad, herring, dogfish (morgy), ling and hake. The heads of the pilchards were left poking out of the pastry at the top, as if gazing up at the stars in thanks, and the tails of the fish poked out of the sides.

Since that day, the same pie has been cooked and enjoyed in Mousehole just before Christmas every year, in celebration of Tom Bawcock and how he saved the village – storm or no storm.

4

A DESPERATE BUSINESS

If you wake at midnight, and hear a horse's feet,
Don't go drawing back the blind, or looking in the street.
Them that ask no questions isn't told a lie.
Watch the wall, my darling, while the Gentlemen go by!

Rudyard Kipling, from Puck of Pook's Hill, *1906*

Here are stories of a coastal English way of life that went on for centuries: smuggling.

During medieval and Tudor times, England's agricultural population grew, and our main export was wool. With the increase in foreign trade opportunities and development of English weaving in the fourteenth century, successive kings demanded export taxes on shipments of English wool abroad. This meant more expense for producers, and also the opportunity to dodge enforcers of the law – and so the 'owlers' were born. These early smugglers took wool out of the country from the Kent and Sussex coast, risking death to avoid paying duties.

Over the following centuries, rising costs – and war after war – meant that taxes increased on all kinds of luxury goods that were exported from, and imported to, England. Each change to the law created new opportunities for smugglers to undercut the official price of goods and ply their trade with foreign contacts. Smugglers didn't mind who they traded with, as long as the money was right. Smuggling expert Richard Platt reports extraordinary sixteenth-century records of cannon and ammunition, made in Forest of Dean foundries, being shipped to Spain by smugglers – these ended up armouring the Spanish Armada that sailed against England in 1588 (see Chapter 6).

The battles between authorities and smugglers took place, of course, on the coast. This is where taxes were levied at the point of goods' exit from, or entry to, the country. Movement of cargo by ship was difficult to hide, but the regulation of customs (import/export duty) by the state only really started in the fifteenth century, and even then it was wholly inadequate. Corruption and collusion with smugglers were rife, and employees were in short supply in wartime. Customs officers had to live within the communities they were supposed to be policing, and that wasn't an easy job.

Smuggling happened all round the English coast, but the short sailing distance to the continent from south-east England meant it was particularly concentrated there. The coming of the Jacobites in the late seventeenth century meant that many smugglers also traded secrets across the Channel, and often enjoyed the active support of local landowners. More anti-smuggling laws were passed, to no avail, yet the duties on goods such as tea and brandy were higher than ever. The stakes escalated rapidly to the point where smuggling gangs, armed and defiant, were prepared for full-blown battles with customs ships to defend their ill-gotten gains. For much of the eighteenth century, smuggling around the coast of England was winning against the British state.

Large-scale smuggling didn't happen just because English people were on the make. In many English communities, life was brutal and short, and poverty was commonplace. The fact that so many people risked their lives in this illegal trade over centuries demonstrates just how desperate they were, and how crippling the state's taxes had become. In the eighteenth century, development of cheaper industry in the north of England hit rural communities hard in the south-east. For the rural poor, smuggling was a way of making ends meet when there was little work to be had. Although all social classes were clearly involved in smuggling, it was usually the poor who did the dangerous work at sea, and faced the consequences.

It was only when the French revolutionary wars created a more intensive military presence on the coast, together with an improvement in the customs and coastguard services, that smuggling by sea began to decline. The 1840s brought a new British free trade policy that drastically reduced import duties and, suddenly, the smuggling trade wasn't worth risking life and limb for. Today, smuggling still continues, in people, drugs and other goods, but it will only happen if economic or other conditions mean it can turn a profit.

Many stories of smuggling in England have survived the centuries. For every tale of a cheeky smuggler tricking his way to riches, there is a story of bloody violence. For every tale of a Mafia-type smuggling network, there is a backdrop of everyday casual crime, just to survive. These stories tell of a craftiness and desperation running through our English national character for generations like a fault line. Some might say it hasn't left us yet.

The Hawkhurst Gang

Sometimes our folk tales can lend an aura of respectability to bad deeds, particularly if those deeds benefit ordinary people and cause discomfort for the rich and powerful. Smuggling is no exception, as the stories in this book demonstrate.

However, real smuggling was rarely a benign activity, and smugglers were not always supported and feted by their communities. In some areas, smuggling gangs held the local people under fear and control, like an eighteenth-century Mafia.

The Hawkhurst Gang emerged in the 1730s as one of the major smuggling networks on the south coast, and certainly the most notorious. Their headquarters was the sleepy hamlet of Hawkhurst in Kent, about 10 miles from the coast, but this bunch of uncompromising thugs were feared all along the south coast from Poole to Folkestone. By the mid-1840s, one of the leaders of the Hawkhurst Gang, Arthur Gray, boasted that if men were needed for a smuggling run, he could assemble 500 of them armed and mounted within an hour for the purpose. They bullied and looted and murdered their way to control smuggling operations over a huge area of the English south coast for a generation.

But all bad things come to an end, eventually. Public outrage at the terrible events in this story, together with the uprising in Goudhurst and other terrible deeds, led to the execution of Gray and his fellow gang leader Thomas Kingsmill in 1748–49 and broke up the Hawkhurst Gang for good.

This folk tale picks up some detail of how the Hawkhurst Gang finally went too far. It's a story that has survived, not because of its humour but because of its horror – it's not for the faint-hearted reader. If you ever travel through the towns and villages in this story, think of the poor souls who were terrorised and sometimes murdered by the vicious Hawkhurst Gang in the 1740s, for few reasons other than greed, gratuitous violence, and being in the wrong place at the wrong time. Also spare a thought for the brave men of Goudhurst, who had enough courage and strategy to stand up to the threats and barbarism of the Hawkhurst Gang and put an end to their terrorism of the sea, England's south coast and its people.

In early 1747, William Sturt was 29 years old and in his prime. He had just returned to his Kent village home of Goudhurst from fighting the French in Ostend, and he craved peace and quiet.

But William was horrified to find crimes of war happening here in his own home county, organised by the villainous gang of smuggling men who used to drink in his local tavern, the Star & Eagle, and originating in Hawkhurst, the larger village to the south.

The good people of Goudhurst were supplying the Hawkhurst Gang with horses, shelter and alibis, in return for scraps of the smuggled loot. They had to, if they knew what was good for them. But then the taxes had been changed and smuggling became less lucrative. Some of the gang were resorting to violent robbery of the local farms and houses around Hawkhurst and Goudhurst. Who would be next?

When his relatives were threatened by a Hawkhurst man, Sturt decided it was time to act. By April, twenty-five men had assembled as the Goudhurst Band of Militia, headed up by Sturt. They were armed with all manner of strange weapons locally to hand from fowling and farming. They were determined to defend their community and, more than that, the authorities had offered a bounty on the heads of the Hawkhurst Gang that was too good to resist.

Even though the Goudhurst rebels tried to keep their existence secret, nothing could be hidden from the Hawkhurst Gang. 'We'll sort them out,' said Thomas Kingsmill, one of the Hawkhurst leaders. 'We'll murder every last man, woman and child of Goudhurst if they try to stop us. Bring it on – let's say the twentieth of April.'

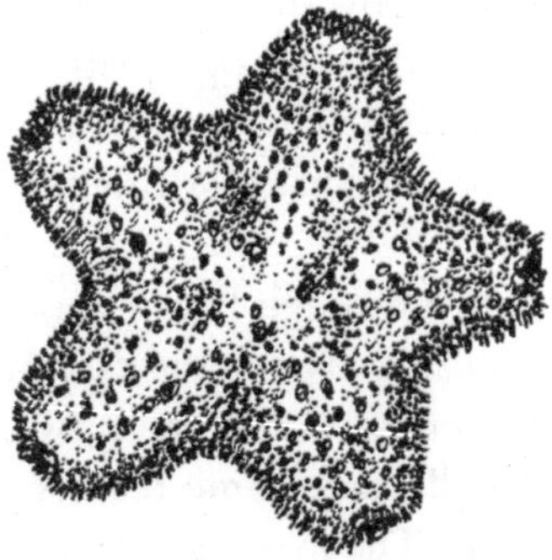

As the day of the great battle approached, women and children left Goudhurst to find safety in the next village. Now here were fifteen men of the Hawkhurst Gang, swaggering into the village stripped to their waists, pistols at the ready and prepared for their appointment.

But they weren't expecting a barrage of bullets fired at them from all quarters as they approached the church. First one smuggler was shot through the heart, then another through the head – and it didn't take many more casualties for the big men to turn on their heels and run away.

The gang were more covert in their operations after that, and nobody could trust anybody else.

In September 1747, the Hawkhurst Gang collaborated with some Dorset smugglers to bring in thirty casks of spirits and 2 tons of tea on a boat from Guernsey. It was due to come into Christchurch Bay, but the boat was intercepted by revenue officers and all the booty was taken to a government warehouse in Poole.

The gangs weren't having that, and they decided to retrieve their goods from the warehouse in the dead of night. On 6 October, they sent scouts into Poole, who returned with the news that naval ships had their guns trained on the customs house. The group waited for the tide to go out, taking the ships as far out as possible, and then thirty armed men broke the place open with strongbars.

The raid was successful. They carried as much as they could back to the horses and rode hard for Brook, about 25 miles away in the New Forest.

As the raiders passed through Fordingbridge, the local people came out of their houses to watch the caravan go by. One of the smugglers noticed a familiar face in the crowd.

'Eh! Young Daniel! Have some tea!' A parcel was thrown towards Daniel Chater. The men rode on in celebratory mood to share out the spoils and disperse.

Back in Fordingbridge, a small crowd gathered around Daniel as if he was a celebrity. 'Who was that?' said one. 'You're not in with that Hawkhurst lot, are you?'

'No, I could never do that,' said Daniel. 'That's old John Diamond. We used to work the harvest at the farm up the road, a few years ago.'

Several weeks later, several government officials walked into Daniel Chater's shoe shop. 'We understand,' said one, 'that you know one of the Hawkhurst Gang.'

'I … I don't know anything,' protested Daniel.

'We'll make it worth your while to talk,' said another official, bringing out a bag of money. 'Your friend Master Diamond is wallowing in Chichester gaol right now. If you can identify him, there's gold in it for you. If you won't, it'll be gaol for you too.'

So on a fateful day in 1748, the shoemaker Daniel Chater set out to Chichester gaol with a customs officer who was carrying an official letter instructing him to take Chater to identify John Diamond. The customs officer's name was William Galley. He'd worked in the same job for years and was considered to be trustworthy for the task.

It was a long and difficult ride from Fordingbridge, and they soon lost their way and had to ask for directions for lodgings for the night. They ended up in the White Hart Inn at Rowland's Castle, which was unfortunate, as the landlady Mrs Payne was a known supporter of smugglers. When she overhead the two men talking over dinner and became suspicious, she sent for William Carter and William Jackson, two members of the Hawkhurst Gang who lived close by.

'We really must be going,' said Galley, getting up. 'Thank you for your hospitality.'

Payne thought quickly. 'I thought you were staying, and I've just locked up the stables for the night. Let me go and see what can be done.' She disappeared for a good while, and by the time she was back, Chater and Galley had company in the bar.

Suddenly the place was packed with men, and Mrs Payne quietly made sure that any innocent potential witnesses were sent away. Jackson bought the two men several drinks and made friendly chit-chat, asking about their purpose; after a little while and a little more liquor, Jackson suggested he had a proposal for Chater and took him outside for a quiet chat.

'You look like you're on official business, a man of your importance,' murmured Jackson. 'You're with friends here, you can tell me what it is.'

'Don't tell,' slurred Chater, 'I'm not proud of it, but I saw them Hawkhursts coming through a few weeks back and they know it. They've made it worth my while, perhaps you should think of doing the same.'

Now here was Galley. 'You're intimidating my witness! I'll have you know I'm the king's man!' Jackson didn't bother replying, he hit Galley in the face and bundled both of them back into the bar. 'Traitors!' roared Jackson, and raised his fist again.

'Stop!' said Mrs Payne. 'I'll not have this kind of behaviour in my place.'

So the smugglers apologised, and soon the drink was flowing again. Daniel Chater and William Galley were soon woozy-headed and both of them retired to their beds.

As they slept, the smugglers crept in and searched their bags. They found the official letter giving instructions to bring Daniel Chater to Chichester as a witness.

With the evidence in their possession, the seven remaining smugglers held a grand council in the bar as they drank. What to do with these two?

'Beat them up good and proper, that'll learn them!' said one.

'Send them to France!' said another.

'Hang them!' said one of the smuggler's wives. 'Hang the bastards, they were going to hang us.'

In the end, the two sleeping men were forced from their beds. With the threat of whips, their hands were tied and they were put on a horse together with their legs tied underneath. The whole smugglers' company set off northwards along a rough country track, and for 5 miles, as the dawn began to show, the two men were whipped and kicked mercilessly as their horse was led forward.

When they got to Lady Holt Park, both men were thrown to the ground.

'Barbarous wretches! For God's sake shoot me through the head or the body!' cried Galley.

'No,' said Jackson, 'we'll make you suffer more yet.'

The company went on in the same fashion. By the time they reached the Red Lion at Rake, Chater was in a bad way and Galley had lost consciousness, falling to the ground. They thought he was dead, and so threw him in the brewhouse, while Chater was chained up in a store.

When the disguise of night fell again that evening, several of the smugglers returned. They dragged Galley, alive or dead, to a fox-hole they had dug into, tipped him in and filled it in with earth.

Chater was left chained in the store for three days before the smugglers took him to a nearby well, attempted to hang him, and then threw his body down a well, with rocks and timbers thrown in afterwards until there was silence.

The murderers had hidden the evidence effectively. Even though the two victims were soon missed, months of searching by the authorities led to nothing. Then an anonymous letter gave the whereabouts of Galley's body; another one followed soon after, naming William Steel as one of the guilty smugglers. When Steel was arrested, he confessed to everything and named all the others involved. Soon all the guilty men had been arrested, imprisoned and tried. Jackson died in prison, some say of fear; the other six were hanged.

Thomas Kingsmill didn't last much longer. He was executed in 1749, following the trial and execution in 1748 of his partner in crime, the foppish financier Arthur Gray.

That was the end of the Hawkhurst Gang.

RED RAGS

This is a sad little story that tells of more desperate times – yet little ones will often try to follow in the footsteps of the adults … It was collected by folklorist Ruth Tongue, and originates from the Isle of Wight in the Napoleonic era, towards the end of the time that large-scale smuggling efforts were commonplace along the south coast of England.

Luggers were working sailboats that were often used for smuggling goods such as spirits, tea and tobacco from France. Bringing a smuggling boat into shore was a tricky operation that needed a number of landing points, lookouts and helpers, usually in the dark of night, and dodging both the revenue cutters and the riding officers on shore. It was a desperate business and violence was everywhere, including guns. This story also shows how the whole community were 'in' on the smuggling game, and how split-second decisions had to be made.

Rags (or tatters) of different colours are a recurring folklore motif in English tradition. They are often tied to trees above magic wells or other sacred spots, as offerings and prayers to the spirits of the place for those who are in need of help.

An island man went to war, leaving his wife with their four small children to bring up the best she could. The eldest boy was very bold and wouldn't ever be stopped, no matter what he wanted to do. And what he wanted most of all was to be a smuggler – on the island, what they used to call an 'owler'.

Before his mother knew anything about it, the boy sneaked aboard a lugger and hid. He travelled all the way to France with them, and he was seasick all the way. The men cursed when they found him. They tried to look after the lad, for they knew whose boy he was.

But on the return journey, just as the lugger was coming back in, the customs cutter fired shots at them and one of the hit the little boy in the arm. The men on board heard him yell, and found him bleeding profusely. They cursed again. One of them ripped up a shirt and tried to stop the bleeding by tying it up the best he could.

This was a bad situation. Any blood on board, not to mention a young lad, with the coastguard on their heels, was more than bad luck; it was a cause for questioning, and they couldn't have it.

There was only one thing for it: one of the men rowed the lad to shore and left him there on the beach, then they took off with their cargo. Soon after that, they successfully dumped their contraband in a safe place. By the time the coastguard caught up with the lugger, and with no trace of boy or blood, the men on board were a picture of innocence.

But when they were safe, I'm sorry to say they didn't go back to find the young lad. They expected him to have already perished there on the beach, or worse still one of the Riding Officers might find him, and his poor mother would have some explaining to do.

So the lad was on the beach in the dark, in a sorry state. But an old woman was watching, an owler's mother, and she got to him before the authorities could. She put the little boy in a pannier on her donkey and covered him in seaweed. She picked up the bloody rags and put them in the other pannier.

Then the old woman rode her donkey up the track to a holy well at the top of the village. It was the kind of place where people would tie rags to the tree branches and make their wishes. She ripped and tore the rags into strips, dark with the little boy's blood, and tied them on to the tree with all the others. The rags were magical wishes for that lad, that he might survive, and also – handily – the evidence of his calamity was safely out of the way.

Just up the track, there was someone from the village searching for the little boy, and so he got carried home to his mother. Whether he survived or not, and whether the wishes at the holy well cast their magic, is another story.

Back down at the beach later that night, the Riding Officer stopped the old woman to search her for smuggled goods. All he found in the donkey's panniers was a load of soggy seaweed.

The Smugglers and the Squire

Lenham is an ancient Kent village, on the southern edge of the South Downs chalk. It's a fairly central point in Kent, halfway along the old main road from Maidstone to Ashford, and so would have made a good distribution centre for smuggled goods brought up from the coast, probably through organised gangs.

Chilston Park is an ancient manor and huge country house (with lakes in the grounds), now a luxury hotel. The records show that most of the squires at Chilston Park during the eighteenth and early nineteenth centuries were also MPs. I wonder whether any of them feature in this story? Sadly, the date of the tale itself isn't recorded; it was reported by Sir Charles Igglesden, editor of the Kentish Express, *in 1925.*

Here is another story that demonstrates strong local support for smuggling, even among the wealthier 'ruling' classes.

Around Lenham there are plenty of old chalk pits near to the old Roman road, and it was here in the old smuggling days that plenty of duty-free goods were hidden. Everyone was in on the act. With the help of the villagers, smugglers would bring their wares here from the coast, and then use the chalk pits as a centre from which to distribute tobacco, spirits, tea and silks to all the people who had money in those parts: lords, farmers and the like. Truth be known, the Justice of the Peace himself couldn't resist a deal in illicit goods. M' learned lord had a nose for good cognac and tobacco, while his wife and daughters loved the fine silk and lace that came from the French ships. Who wouldn't?

One nasty, rainy night, the smugglers were hefting barrels of their merchandise up from the coast to the chalk pits, when they were rumbled by revenue officers. Those officials gave chase, and the smugglers were properly on the run with the handicap of all their precious loot, in the pouring rain as well. They were on the track that passed Chilston Park when one of them had an idea.

'Quick, in here! The squire will help us.'

It just so happened that at that time, the squire at Chilston Park was having a big lake dug out and lined with clay. With the discipline of an ex-sailor, he was employing continuous labour with a night watch. The smugglers ran into the estate and up to the big house and asked to see the man of the house.

As soon as the squire heard from the smugglers of their predicament, he knew the action that was needed. The barrels were thrown into the glooping mud of the new lake and covered, and the smugglers took off their coats, picked up spades and joined the gang of labourers digging in the downpour.

When the revenue officers came calling, all was quiet at Chilston Park apart from the thud of the labourers' spades, the steady patter of rain, and the bark of commands from the squire.

The revenue officers doffed their caps politely. 'Have the likes of smugglers passed this way, m' lud?'

'No,' said the squire, and of course he was telling the truth; the smugglers hadn't passed by, they were straight under the noses of the revenue officers there and then, trying desperately not to giggle.

The officers left to continue their search, the barrels were dug out of the mud in the pouring rain, and the squire was declared a hero.

For many years after that, to toast the anniversary of the event, the squire would find a new barrel of fine cognac miraculously appear in the cellar of his grand house.

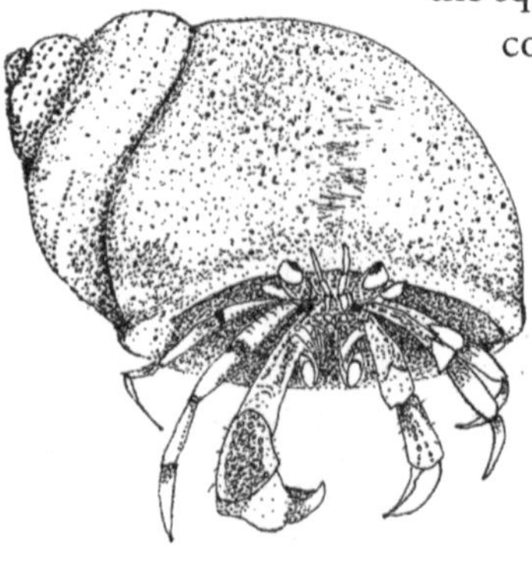

BESSIE CATCHPOLE

This is a rare story of a female smuggler from Harwich. Derived from the Rev. Forbes Phillips' 1909 The Romance of Smuggling, *it makes me wonder about the largely untold stories of women in the smuggling racket over the centuries.*

History doesn't record the name of Bessie Catchpole's husband. We do know that he was either careless or unlucky, because he got caught out. Master Catchpole was on board his little ship the *Sally* one night, on his way back laden with brandy and tobacco, when he was caught in the fire from the customs men and he died.

That didn't deter Bessie Catchpole. She took her husband's ship, she took his breeches and his pipe and she took his job – and she wore all of them like she had been smuggling all her life.

On board the *Sally*, she waved her husband's cutlass at the crew. 'I'm the captain now,' she said. 'You'll obey my orders now.'

'Right you are, Bessie,' said each one of them, as she stood and stared hard at them, until she got the response she wanted.

The last one, the youngest of the ship's lads, stifled a chuckle, and that set them all off laughing until he got a fine right hook on the jaw from Bessie that knocked him out cold.

They didn't laugh at her again.

For the next two years, it was Bessie who managed the smuggling runs of that little ship, to and from Holland and France. One night, though, a revenue cutter was chasing their ship and it would have caught them, but the wind suddenly (luckily) dropped.

She signalled to the crew, and silently they took each of the brandy kegs on board and sank them in the sea. Then they waited.

At dawn, the revenue men rowed their boats out to the *Sally* in a very bad mood. 'We've been searching for your bloody ship all night,' they said. 'Right, let's see what you've got on board here.'

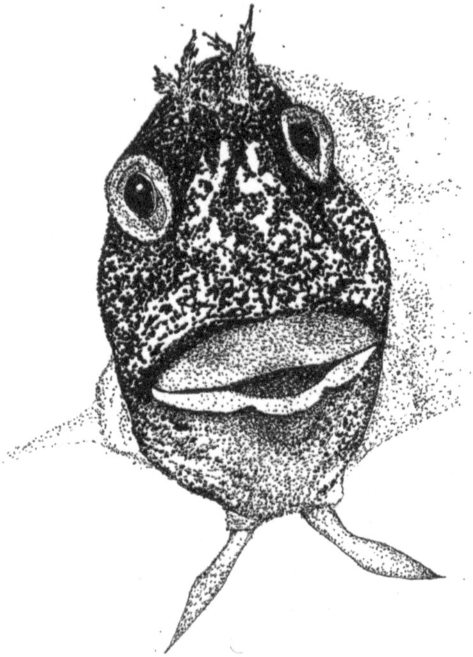

They found nothing. The revenue officer faced Bessie with a frown.

'Why were you running away, if there was nothing to hide on this ship?' he demanded.

'If I'd known it was you,' said Bessie with a winning smile, 'I would have waited. But not all of the king's officers are so handsome.'

Later that day, with the revenue officers well out of the way, Bessie and her men drank the king's health with the brandy they'd dredged up.

'At least I didn't hoist the yellow handkerchief,' said Bessie. 'That would have meant we were a plague ship. We'll try that next time.'

Smuggler's Leap

Smugglers in Devon found the north of the county presented a more challenging coast than the many bays of south Devon. The north has long stretches of rocky foreshore and the current of the Bristol Channel to contend with, both of which lent themselves more naturally to wrecking. Apart from Lundy (see Chapter 6), the best coast in north Devon for a spot of smuggling was between Lynmouth and Ilfracombe.

One report of customs officers from here, dated 23 June 1786, recorded 'three hampers containing sixty-six bottles of gin, about thirteen gallons red Portugal wine, about two hundred and fifty pounds white salt, and one box with seventy-three packs playing cards without the ace of spades, seized in the outhouse of John Beer at Lee'. There's more than a few stories in that report.

Here's an image to finish my smugglers' tales: a desperate leap into the unknown.

Above Lee Bay, near Lynmouth, the road climbs steeply along the cliffs to Martinhoe. From this road, a steep rocky path leads down to the locally named Sandy Cove, where the smugglers brought in their illicit goods, and the precipice here is called Smuggler's Leap.

Once a notorious smuggler was riding to Martinhoe along this stretch of road, hotly pursued by a revenue officer. The official had a much better horse, and the smuggler was in grave danger of being caught.

Just as the smuggler reached the rocky precipice, the revenue officer rode alongside him and reached out to capture his prey. In a last desperate move, the smuggler swerved his horse towards the cliff's edge. The poor beast lost its balance and plunged right over the edge, carrying the smuggler with it.

The smuggler scrabbled furiously at anything that could save him, and clutched at the official, dragging him from the saddle. The two men, still fighting each other, both fell to their deaths on the rocks below. Even when their bodies were eventually found, those two were still locked in battle.

5

RAVENING MONSTERS

Below the thunders of the upper deep,
Far, far beneath in the abysmal sea,
His ancient, dreamless, uninvaded sleep
The Kraken sleepeth.

Alfred, Lord Tennyson (1809–92)

If you were a sizeable monster wanting a bit of peace and quiet from pesky humans, where would you hide? The sea, of course.

Ever since Aristotle's time, human society has been thrilled, disturbed and horrified by tales of huge sea creatures. The surface of the ocean could conceal a hundred hungry sea serpents lurking in the deep, among other horrors real or imagined.

Many of the reports of monsters from England's coastline could be explained away as the sightings of actual sea creatures – for example whales, or even the 8m-long giant oarfish. Many of the monsters in our stories and anecdotes appear somewhat benign, which would fit the profile of giant plankton-feeding creatures. There are stories of oarfish coming to the surface in numbers just before deep-sea tremors or tsunamis, thereby acting as a kind of warning system.

But the powers of our imaginations to generate sea monsters reach far beyond the limits of marine biology. Here is a selection of mysterious coastal and marine creatures that have taken form in English folk tale. Some of these monsters are friendly and some of them are definitely hungry for human trouble.

SEA SERPENTS AND SEA SNAKES

The notion of a sea serpent seems very ancient, and there have been sightings of such creatures regularly recorded through the ages all around the British coast. Like so many short snippets of folk tales, the fragments of story that have survived are matter of fact but tantalising in their lack of detail.

These little tales give a flavour of the ways in which our ancestors dealt with such creatures, both in folk tale and history. The first is a local version of a tale found in tribes all over the world, recorded by folklorist Ruth Tongue in 1947. The second, of sea monsters seen off the East Yorkshire coast, is one example of many such contemporary sightings of sea monsters all around the English coast. Finally, the case of the Morgawr at Falmouth demonstrates how folklore and folk tradition can begin in modern times, not always originating in actual fact.

There used to be a sea serpent that would swim all the way up the Solway Firth and eat everything in sight – not only the fish, but the fishermen and the fowlers too, even the cattle that would come down to the shore to eat the seaweed. Because of the greed of this great monster, the people starved – those that were left.

So they decided to take action to save themselves. They cut a hundred hazel stakes with sharpened ends, and they went out in their little coracles at low tide and drove the blunt end of every stake into the mud of the Solway Firth, so the spikes stuck up – but just below the tide, so the water covered them when it came back in.

Everyone ran home to safety, and then the tide came in.

The great, greedy worm came in with the tide, and it got well and truly stuck on those spikes; all hundred of them pierced right through it like a pincushion. It took it three days to die, the tide coming in and out all the time, and how that monster bellowed with the pain of it!

But the people were wise enough to leave the great creature to its death – it had caused them so much trouble.

Then it finally died, and the gulls and the fish had a grand feed, but the people wouldn't touch the loathsome thing.

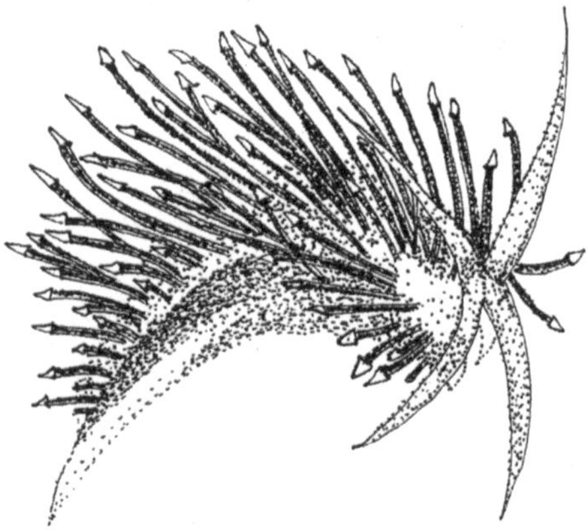

In August 1931, the stream trawler *Chandos* reported a curious sighting off the coast east of Hull, at Spurn Point. Looking inshore, the boatmen had observed the brown sails of two boats. But as they sailed closer, it was plain these were not boats at all. They were looking at the dorsal fins of two huge sea creatures, which moved away at speed. Later, the boatmen estimated the creatures were about 50ft long, and unlike anything they had ever seen before.

They were the first of many to see monsters in the North Sea. Suddenly, monsters were everywhere, all along the coast from Spurn Point to Whitby and everywhere in between. In 1934, Thomas Atkinson and his wife and children even encountered the creature in the Humber at Hull, where the beast 'turned to gaze at them with eyes as great as portholes'.

To top it all, soon after, Thomas Sheppard, the curator of Hull's museum, told the *Mail* that he had found footprints of the giant sea creature in the sand at Spurn Point. Surely here was a man of knowledge to be trusted!

Sadly, the truth of the matter was that Sheppard's waste-paper basket, made of a hollowed-out elephant's foot, had been used by Sheppard himself to make the prints.

If you go to Hull's museum today you can still see the waste paper basket (please do think about the poor elephant too). You might also be lucky enough to spy the real monster if you gaze on the grey North Sea for long enough. For who is to say those first reports weren't true?

Morgawr means 'sea giant' in Cornish. It has also come to refer to the celebrated sea monster of Falmouth Bay and the Helford River in Cornwall. There have been reports of sea monsters here for many centuries, but for some reason one particular great monster decided to hang out in this area in the 1970s.

The first sighting, off Pendennis Point in September 1975, was of a 'hideous humped creature with a long, bristled neck and stumpy horns' which was seen catching and eating a conger eel.

Early in 1976, a mysterious woman calling herself 'Mary F' sent photographs to the local newspaper, *The Falmouth Packet*, of a monster in the sea off Falmouth. These images suggested that monster was suspiciously Nessie-like, and the accompanying letter claimed darkly that the beast 'moved in a funny way', and that 'My brother developed the films, I didn't want to take it to the chemist.'

The next sighting, in July 1976, was from two fishermen, George Vinnecombe and John Cock, who spied a capsized boat in the water and went to investigate, only to find it wasn't a boat. 'It looked like a prehistoric monster,' they said. 'We've got a 32ft boat, and it was as big as our boat.'

Through the roasting hot summer of 1976 and the years beyond, Falmouth went monster mad. Scientists, new-agers, media and tourists all flocked to the south Cornwall town hoping for their own sighting of the great creature. Television programmes were made and schoolchildren imagined what the monster might look like. The trouble was, they all had about as much hope of seeing a monster off the coast there as anywhere else on the shores of Britain, for the Morgawr was an elaborate prank.

Tony 'Doc' Shiels was an artist, street performer and self-proclaimed 'Wizard of the West', who also constructed another new folk myth, that of the 'Owl Man', in 1976. Together with Noel Wain, a writer for the *Falmouth Packet*, it is likely that Shiels produced the infamous 'Mary F' photographs of the Morgawr along with other tall tales and even rituals to summon the monster and keep it in the public eye. Folklorist Ronald M. James suggests that Shiels and Wain's 'prank' (some might call it an artistic act) has inspired real belief in the Morgawr, not just as a folk tradition but in reality.

But what about all the other sightings of monsters from Falmouth since that time? Have they been pranks too, or have they actually happened?

THE GIANT OF GRABBIST

These tall tales of a friendly giant were reported by Somerset folklorist Ruth Tongue, based on her recollections from the early part of the twentieth century. I am not sure how authentic they are, but they're great fun. They convey something of the hidden landscapes of west Somerset and the eastern part of Exmoor, so close to the coast. Grabbist Hill and the 'purple coloured mountain' area around Dunster is one of the places that may have inspired the hymn All Things Bright and Beautiful, *written by Cecil Frances Alexander in 1848.*

Grabbist is an Iron Age hill fort, easily walkable from Dunster. Just below the fort is a depression in the ground, caused naturally by land slippage, known as the Giant's Chair. The site is a Scheduled Ancient Monument now owned by the National Trust. Around the hill is a stunning landscape of ancient woodland, heathland and grassland that is home to a number of special and rare species; however, I have found no modern records of the giant. Battlegore is another prehistoric site: a Bronze Age burial chamber at Williton, gloriously named after a Danish raid in the tenth century.

There was a rare giant in Somerset. He walked all the way from Cornwall, and there he was in Dunster.

The people of Exmoor were more than a bit scared that a giant had turned up on their doorstep, but over the coming weeks they realised they needn't have worried. All their sheep and cattle were still there, there was no violence, and no roaring; the giant didn't cause problems for anyone at all, and he seemed to disappear from the moor for most of the day.

Someone piped up in the pub one day and asked, 'What does that old giant eat? Is he getting enough food?'

An old fellow from Porlock said sagely, 'He likes fish.'

The giant had been going out to the coast. Every morning, it seemed, he would wade out into the Bristol Channel, scooping up handfuls of fish as he went. All the fishing boats had to do was wait and he would load their decks with fish, and then they could all go home again by the middle of the morning and leave the giant to eat fish in peace. So everyone was happy.

One morning, a ship called the *Dorcas Jane* came along for the giant's fish festival. She was a lovely old creaking ship, and her captain was called Elijah Crowcombe. That morning, the *Dorcas Jane* was loaded up with fish scooped out of the sea by the giant, and the boat turned for home well-laden. But out of nowhere, a great storm whipped up and the waves around the boat were soon 10ft tall. Elijah realised they were further out in the Channel than they should be, and it would be impossible to steer the boat to safety. All of the sailors were crying and praying for their lives, when out of the lashing rain and the howling wind came two great giant's hands. He picked up the *Dorcas Jane* as though it was a little toy boat, and before the men on ship could even say 'Thank you!' he very gently put the boat down in the relative calm of Watchet harbour. Then away he strode, back over to Dunster.

Everyone grew quite fond of their giant, and they would wave to him if they saw him striding back from the sea along the river. He'd sit on top of Dunster hill, with feet on either side of the castle, and wash all the salt off his legs. Then he'd stride away to his hiding place at Grabbist, and everyone along the way knew that if they waved at him and he waved back, their washing would dry on the line.

So the people of neighbouring Hawkridge decided to build a church, and the giant agreed to help them lift the rocks up from the coast to make the walls. But the Devil saw what was going on, and he didn't like it.

Next time the giant was striding up from the coast with his arms all full of rocks and stones, the Devil went and stuck his foot out in front of the giant and tripped him up proper. The stones went everywhere, and where the stones fell, great crashes and howls went up from the humans all around.

The giant was a kindly soul and he didn't lose his temper. He just quietly picked up all the dropped stones and carried them to the place where they were building a church, and there he put them carefully down where they were needed, one by one.

Then the giant found one stone that was all cracked and broken, and he didn't like that, so he threw it aside. It just happened to land with a THUMP! right next to where the Devil was sitting, and the Devil had to move himself sharpish.

Once the church was built, the giant used the rest of the rocks to make a line in the river, and that became the Tarr Steps over the River Barle.

The Devil shouted up at the giant. 'There's only room for one of us here, and it isn't you. Let's have a contest.'

'All right,' said the giant.

'Let's see who can throw a stone the furthest. We'll start here on Bossington Beacon and throw over there, towards Porlock Common.'

The Devil threw his stone first, and he threw it a full 4 miles, all the way to Porlock Common.

The giant picked up his stone to try and throw it further, but just before he threw, the Devil stuck his leg out again and tripped the giant up. So the giant's stone landed about 3ft behind the Devil's stone.

The Devil laughed out loud, but the giant said nothing; he just sat on the Devil. Sat down right on top of him, and squashed him flat. The Devil squirmed and wriggled, but the giant didn't care. He got his pipe, and stuffed it with tobacco, and sat and smoked and smoked until all the tobacco was gone.

Then the giant got up and took hold of the Devil's tail between his finger and thumb. He peered closely at the infernal face. 'THAT wasn't fair,' said the giant. 'We will throw stones again, on the Quantocks, but, in the meantime, I think you should go and cool down.'

The Devil squealed and squealed, but the giant kept hold of his tail and whirled the Devil round his head once, twice, three times, and threw him out over Porlock Bay, right out into the Bristol Channel, where he landed with a splosh! and a hiss!

Then the giant smiled to himself and walked home to Dunster. On the way, he found a little foal all stuck in the mud, but he pulled it out, rubbed the mud off it very gently, and gave it back to its mother. Good deeds done for the day, the giant was away for a snooze.

The giant did meet the Devil again soon after that, for another contest up by West Quantock. This time the giant went first, and he hurled his stone miles and miles away until it landed at Battlegore.

'Now you throw,' he said to the Devil. 'Fairly.'

The Devil was fuming at this, and he was so angry that he couldn't concentrate on his stone. So his throw was more than a bit rubbish, and not a patch on the giant's.

The giant snorted.

'So,' he said, 'I win. YOU must promise to leave this place and these good people, and never come back, d' you hear? I'll give you a head start.'

The giant picked up the Devil by his ear this time, squealing and yelling, and he waded all the way out to the middle of the Bristol Channel, until he was right up to his armpits.

Then the giant swung the Devil round and round his head until he was dizzy, before he let go and the Devil flew so far away he landed in the middle of the Atlantic Ocean.

He had a long way to swim back, that old Devil. When he did eventually make it back to shore, he never returned to Somerset, making sure he stayed well clear of that giant.

Look carefully, because maybe he's still there … somewhere. If a giant could ever hide in the English landscape, it would be in west Somerset.

The Laidly Worm of Spindlestone Heughs

This story is set on a dramatic and magical part of the Northumbrian coast, close to the Farne Islands and steeped in history. The coastline here is now designated Site of Special Scientific Interest (SSSI) for its geological and botanical interest.

King Ida of Bernicia (AD c.547–c.559*), who ultimately began the kingdom of Northumbria, founded Bamburgh Castle on the site of a Celtic fort, perched on Whin Sill crag overlooking the North Sea. Several versions of the castle have followed, and it has been captured by Britons, Anglo-Saxons, Vikings and Normans in turn. It's possible to visit and even stay in the castle today. Nearby Spindlestone Heughs is also part of the Whin Sill rock formation. The Spindle Stone or Bridle Rock is a distinctive crag that features in some versions of the Laidly Worm story, where the prince threw his bridle before meeting the dragon. Nearby 'Worm Cave' has sadly long since been quarried away.*

England's fairy tales are usually land-lubber's affairs, and it is rare for the sea to feature in them. First published in a book of folk songs in 1778, The Ballad of the Laidly Worm of Spindlestone Heughs *was composed by the Rev. Robert Lambe, the vicar of Norham, who claimed ancient sources for the tale. There are certainly some similarities to Scottish and Icelandic folk tale motifs, including the Child ballads 'Kemp Owyne' and 'The Laily [sic] Worm and the Mackerel of the Sea' where both son and daughter are transformed by the queen – one into a dragon and the other into a fish. In some versions of the tale, the prince is called 'Childe Wynde', meaning noble youth.*

Classic versions of this dramatic fairy tale tend to paint its characters in bold, cliched brush strokes: the evil stepmother; the absent father; the innocent damsel in distress; and the brave hero/saviour. Working with the tale as a modern storyteller, my version has turned out a little differently. Here are tensions arising from a change in family dynamics, which if left unchecked can turn into extreme bullying. Throw some magic into the mix (who is monstering whom?), together with love, and it all gets very interesting indeed.

I love the motifs of rowan wood and red cord for the boat in this story, both of which give magical protection to counter and repel malevolent magic. Worm, or wyrm, is the old word for dragon. 'Heugh' is a local word for crag or cliff.

A long time ago, when Bamburgh Castle was still a fine building fit for royalty, a king and queen lived there with their two children: a prince and a princess.

When the two children were on the cusp of adulthood, the prince (as princes did) went to seek his fortune away from home, and test his mettle through travel and adventure. But princesses were expected to stay at home and wait for the right marriage.

The next springtime, the queen fell ill. Despite all the attempts of the royal physicians to heal her, she died. The household was cloaked in grief, and although the king could busy himself with royal duties, the princess had little to occupy her time. So the whole court took the princess to their hearts, and nothing was too much trouble for her; anything to bring a smile and some cheer.

Two years passed, and the king went away hunting for a few days. This was nothing unusual, but this time when he returned, he brought a beautiful woman with him, and introduced her to the princess. 'My dear daughter, we have great good fortune. This wonderful lady has agreed to be my wife and queen. I am sure you will welcome her with open arms.'

The princess wasn't very impressed at this, as no woman could take the place of her mother, but for her father's sake, she tried very hard. For a couple of months, the princess and her new stepmother were very polite to one another and tried to keep the peace, peering at each other when they thought the other wasn't looking. But true feelings have a way of showing themselves, eventually.

Everyone at court was quite enchanted by this fiery, theatrical, intelligent new queen. The princess felt ignored and discarded, as everyone was paying more attention to the new queen than to her, including her father. She began to complain – loudly – to the king that her stepmother was a horrible woman, and she did everything she could to undermine and outshine the queen at every opportunity.

Her stepmother, for her part, began to show irritation with every little thing the princess did. Nothing was ever good enough: the princess was always in the way; and the young girl found herself excluded and ignored. But she couldn't be angry, because princesses aren't meant to behave like that. She hid in her room away from everyone.

'She's a witch!' sobbed the princess.

'She's a threat to the kingdom!' cried the new queen.

'Why can't you two women just get along with each other?' sighed the king. 'I'm staying out of this.'

That same night the queen decided to take action. Did I say she was wise? In secret, hidden in the dungeon of Bamburgh Castle, she pounded herbs and resins in a mortar and burned them as she chanted her incantations, three times, six times, nine times. Here's what she said:

I weird you to be a Laidly Worm,
And free shall you never be,
Until the King's own son
Comes to the Heugh and gives you kisses three;
And that could never ever be.

The princess went to bed that night feeling unsettled, but eventually she managed to drift off to sleep.

The next morning, when her ladies came into the princess's chamber to dress her, instead of a young woman in the bed, they found a dreadful, reeking dragon, the Laidly Worm, uncoiling itself to attack. As they ran screaming from the room, the worm slithered and crawled its way down the stairs, through the hallway and out into the open air. It slithered and crawled its way across grass and rock and heath until it reached the Spindlestone rock, where it coiled itself round three times and snoozed.

Everyone in the surrounding country soon knew of the Laidly Worm at Spindlestone Heughs, as the monster scoured the land for food, devouring most creatures in its path, big or small, human or animal. The creature was all-powerful for miles around, scorching the earth with its anger and making everything uninhabitable. It threatened the whole kingdom.

The king was distraught. What had happened to his daughter – and where had this dreadful monster come from? What was to be done?

At last, the king sent for a wise man who lived below the cliffs, and asked for his advice. The wise man muttered incantations of his own into the fire and looked gravely at the king.

'The dragon must not be slain, because it is actually the princess under a great enchantment,' he said. 'She is hungry, and angry at her situation, for which you cannot blame her. The only thing that will break this enchantment, and throw it back to the one who created it, is your son the prince, her brother. Send over the seas for him. In the meantime, every day as the sun goes down, have a stone trough filled with the milk of seven cows, and this will bring the dragon some peace for the while.'

All was done as the wise man advised. The milk calmed the dragon's temper a little and nobody else was killed. They sent abroad for the prince, and when he heard the news he swore a binding oath to rescue her from her plight, no matter what it took.

The prince set to work with the advice of his own magicians. He had a longboat built that was all made of rowan wood, and the ropes of the boat were all bright red. When all was ready to the prince's satisfaction, he and his men set out with their oars and pulled sheer for Bamburgh Keep.

The clouds were stormy as the ship approached, and the stepmother was on the lookout. Again, she worked her magic and quickly summoned spirits to wreck the boat. 'He must never land!' she cried. 'Raise the gales! Push his wretched boat against the rocks! Bring the Laidly Worm down to the shore to attack him!'

But when her spirits got near to the boat, they found it protected against them by the wood of the rowan tree and the red cords. All the spirits could do was glance off the longboat into the angry skies. The Laidly Worm crawled down to the shore from its coiling stone, and waited by the harbour.

The boat was close now, but every time it tried to come in, the great worm lashed its tail in the water and caused huge waves to rock the boat to oblivion. 'Hold oars!' shouted the prince, 'steady her!' The third wave nearly sent the boat on to its side, and so the prince ordered that they should row out to the ocean again, and the stepmother, watching from the castle, thought she had won the day.

But the boat simply rounded the next point and landed safely in Budle Creek. Then, all with swords and bows at the ready, they scrambled over land to tackle the terrible worm. As he ran, the prince wondered what he would find; he did not want to be killed by a dragon-sister, but neither did he want to kill or wound her. He didn't know that when his feet touched land, the magic cast by his stepmother was already weakened.

As the prince approached the worm with sword drawn, the Laidly Worm was docile and did not try to attack him. He crept closer, all the time fearing for his life, all the time ready to strike if he needed to. He was close enough now to touch its hideous, stinking hide, and then the voice of his own sister came from the dragon's mouth:

Cast your sword and bow aside,
And give me kisses three;
For though I am a poisonous worm,
No harm I'll do to thee.

The prince stayed his hand. Could he trust this voice, or was it a false enchantment? Then came the voice again:

Cast your sword and bow aside,
And give me kisses three,
If I'm not won by set of sun,
Won never shall I be.

There was nothing else to do. The prince gingerly went up to the great head of the dragon and kissed it once on the mouth.

Nothing happened. He took a second aside to breathe away from the stench, then kissed the creature again. Still nothing happened. Trying not to retch, the prince kissed the dragon for a third time on the mouth, and there was a loud hissing sound. The hide of the dragon collapsed and shrivelled in front of him, and there standing in front of him was his sister the princess, still in her nightgown, looking a little embarrassed.

The prince wrapped his cloak around her and they walked up to the castle. The king ran to meet them, and took them up to the topmost room of the castle tower where a small crowd had gathered.

'The queen was standing here one minute,' said the king, 'then the next minute, all there was on the floor was this warty old toad.'

The toad glowered at them with its coppery eyes and tried to crawl away.

'No escaping,' said the prince. 'This is the queen's own magic rebounded on to her, and this is her punishment. She will be a loathsome toad for the same number of days as my sister was a dragon, and she will hide in her room in the castle and be ignored by everyone.'

It came to pass, exactly as the prince had predicted.

When the toad changed back into a queen at the end of her allotted time, what happened then?

The queen and the princess had to make their peace with one another and find a way to be friends, of course.

That's magic for you.

HOW FILEY BRIGG CAME TO BE

Filey Brigg is a long, narrow headland on the north Yorkshire coast just above Filey. It's a protected site because of its geology and birdlife.

There are two stories about how Filey Brigg came to exist. The true story is that it was formed by a landslip because of the different kinds of rocks present in the area – but that's not quite as compelling, is it?

The Devil story may have come about because of the danger for boats coming too close to the Brigg. Similar stories about the markings on fish, and the Devil's work in causing problems for sailors, can be found in other parts of Britain and beyond.

The dragon story was heard in Somerset, from a young Yorkshire groom, sometime around 1905, and recorded decades later by Ruth Tongue. It features one of the finest cakes known to England: parkin.

A 'blackjack' is a leather tankard, sealed with tar on the inside. A 'drashel' is a threshold. A 'hod-me-dod' is the local word for a snail. 'Vittles' is the old vernacular for 'victuals' or food.

The Devil made Filey Brigg, and the Devil makes sure it gets in the way of boats and ships and causes danger for everyone to this day.

When the Devil was making Filey Brigg, he dropped his hammer into the sea, and he groped around in the water for it. He didn't find the hammer, but he did catch a fish with his bare hands. It was a haddock.

Disgusted, the Devil threw it back into the sea, but he left scorch marks on either side of the haddock's head. The poor creature still bears those markings today.

Once in a gully near Filey there lived a great dragon. Everyone in the village kept away from the dragon, quite sensibly, apart from Mrs Greenaway, who lived in a little cottage up on the hill overlooking the gully. Mrs Greenaway was one of those cunning women who was good with herbs, and charms, and problems – everyone reckoned she would be quite all right living up there, dragon or no dragon, and so she was.

The grass up on the hill above the gully was growing well in the springtime, but the farmers decided to move their cows and sheep over the hill towards the village. For who wanted to fatten up animals, only to have them eaten by a dragon?

So the dragon was a hungry dragon – it had few animals to eat of any substance, and no nice plump farmers to eat either.

On the other side of the gully, high on the hill, lived Billy Biter the travelling tailor, still in the same cottage he had grown up in. All the villagers liked Billy Biter, and his old mother who lived with him. Everyone warned them it was no good living so close to a dragon, but then everyone did their best to look after those two stuck out in a little cottage on the hill. So they were all right.

Those were good times, and there was always a warm welcome at the Biters' little cottage, with a warm fire in the hearth and the kettle boiling merrily above it, and the old puss-cat washing itself in the corner. When Billy was away on his travels, everyone went up there to help, bringing in logs and hauling up fresh water for the old lady and, from over the gully, Mrs Greenaway kept an eye out for the old dear too.

But when old Mrs Biter died, things took a turn for the worse.

Poor little Billy was all on his own and lonesome, but then he went and got married, to a proper fright of a woman. Hepzibah was her name, and she was 6ft tall and thin as a yard of pump water, while Billy was short and plump-ish, but that wasn't the worst of it.

Hepzibah didn't drink much of that pump water. She was always tipping drink down her gullet from her great blackjack.

The villagers reckoned that she had only married Billy because the little cottage was half a mile from the pub, and that Hepzibah had scared Billy into it. She tipped drink down her neck whenever she could, while it was Billy who had to get the firewood and the water, make the home all cosy and get the kettle on, before he went out looking for Hepzibah. Billy took his wheelbarrow, because sometimes she would still be in the pub, but sometimes he'd find her bedraggled and sleeping by the side of the track, her blackjack empty, and she would need hauling home. On other days, she made it back to the cottage and would sleep in Mrs Biter's old rocking chair by the fire, and her all snoring and drooling from the drink. If Hepzibah woke up, she would be in a foul mood, and she would chase poor Billy round the kitchen and threaten him with the broom handle. So, on those nights, Billy and the tom-cat both used to tiptoe past Hepzibah's chair and out into the night, and they would curl up around the chimney of the cottage for a bit of warmth and a bit of peace and quiet.

So it went on, day after day and week after week, until one day Billy was out and about and he met Mrs Greenaway.

'Where's your pay money, Billy?' said Mrs Greenaway, looking at him directly.

'Why, it's here,' muttered Billy, reaching into his pocket and bringing out some old coppers.

'I can give you something in return for those coins,' said Mrs Greenaway, and she gave him a silver sixpence.

Billy Biter began to feel much better. He went home and gave Hepzibah the silver sixpence; later that evening, she was in such a terrible temper that Billy and the cat crept out and curled up around the chimney pot out on the roof.

Watching from the other side of the gully, Mrs Greenaway noticed that the smoke coming from the chimney of the little cottage stopped by and by, and it was all in darkness. She also heard the dragon, whose hungry growl echoed around the valley, but he didn't show himself that night.

The next day, the same things happened. Mrs Greenaway gave Billy a full silver sixpence, and he felt stronger; that night, Hepzibah was out cold sprawled across the drashel, so Billy and the cat stepped over her and went and spent the night on the roof in the rain. The dragon roared his hunger from the valley again, but he didn't do much about it.

On the third day, Billy visited the local farmer, whose wife fed him a slap-up Yorkshire tea before sending him on his way. He tried to stash a little bit of food in his pocket for the tom-cat, but the farmer's wife saw it and roared with laughter. 'We're all very fond of you, Billy, you know,' she said, 'and you don't dance and sing nearly enough these days. Here – I'll pack up some vittles for you to last into this evening and tomorrow too. They will need cooking up, but maybe Hepzibah will do that for once?' She filled his bag full to the top with flour, and eggs, and milk, and oatmeal, and honey, and molasses, and ginger, and tied a good dry faggot of wood on to that. The farmer and his wife watched Billy Biter walking off into the trees with a load on his back enough for a wheelbarrow; he was going as slow as a hod-me-dod.

Nevertheless, Billy made good enough time through the woods, but then he smelt cooking and he followed his nose like an old hod-me-dod to old Mrs Greenaway's cottage.

She came to the door. 'Come in, Billy Biter, and all your vittles and firewood too: Hepzibah won't be needing them, but I will, a poor old lady like me,' and she took them off him. Billy's eyes were huge as he looked longingly at the food, but he knew he shouldn't say anything as Mrs Greenaway had helped him so much.

Mrs Greenaway didn't even bother to undo the parcels, she just shook something like flour over them. 'I've been baking parkin,' she said. 'Can you smell it?'

Billy could smell nothing but the delicious parkin baking in the oven. (The dragon, way below in the gully, could smell it too. But we'll come to that.)

Mrs Greenaway smiled. 'I'll give you some parkin to warm your belly on the way home,' she said, and cut a huge slice from the tin. 'A bit for your puss-cat as well … And this corner here, that's for Hepzibah alone – *make sure nobody else has that corner*, mind,' and she looked at Billy sternly until he nodded.

So Billy Biter got loaded up again with all the vittles and the faggot of firewood, and Hepzibah's corner of parkin wrapped in fresh leaves and placed on top of the lot. But he wasn't going as slow as he had done before. He was full of hope – perhaps even Hepzibah might take it on herself to cook them some decent food tonight! – and even better, he had his own great slice of parkin to nibble at in the meantime. Life was good!

No wonder, then, that Billy Biter took a wrong step, and then another one. He lost his balance on the mossy ground and went headlong down into the gully – right into the place where the dragon lived, in among all the red-hot rocks surrounding the beast itself. He landed right on top of the load on his back, and up against a red light that blinked with surprise in the gloom.

'Let's have a proper look at ye,' said the dragon, 'so I can see what I'm about to eat.'

Billy's knees knocked and his teeth chattered, and he dropped his slice of parkin right in front of the dragon's nose.

The dragon sniffed. 'What's that then?' Out came the lolling tongue of the dragon and whipped that parkin right into its mouth.

'P-p-p-parkin,' stammered Billy Biter.

The dragon made a disgusting sound when he was chewing. 'This is good parkin,' he said. 'Get me some more.'

Then, as a crumb went up its nose, the dragon sneezed. That sneeze blew Billy Biter and his bag of vittles up into the gully, high in the air, and he landed on the cold roof of his own cottage, with the puss-cat clinging to the chimney for dear life. The rope on his bag was so scorched from the dragon that it broke, and the contents of all the parcels came rattling down the chimney – thump-thump-thump! – into the embers of the hearth, just missing Hepzibah, who was sprawled on the hearthside with her dress all tattered and her empty blackjack alongside her. Her own big corner of parkin came to a stop just by her nose.

Hepzibah sniffed, and she snorted, and her eyelids flickered open. She grabbed the parkin and gobbled it down, and then looked about her.

'Billy Biter!' she roared up the chimney, 'come down here! Throwing bits of cake around. What is it, anyway?'

'P-p-p-parkin,' stammered Billy, climbing down from the roof very carefully. (The cat stayed where it was.)

'Parkin!' bellowed Hepzibah. 'I'll show you how to make proper parkin!'

And she did. Billy had to salvage all the ingredients that were left, and Hepzibah kicked and trampled the dough in a pig trough until she was satisfied it was ready. Then she threw a big round dollop of mixture on to a baking sheet and shoved it in the oven.

By this time, Billy had retreated back to the roof again. 'Parkin's meant to be square, not round,' he whispered to the cat. 'But I'm not telling her.'

In only two minutes, the parkin was ready – and that's not right, is it? The parkin was cooked and round and rich and sticky, and Hepzibah held it up in triumph. 'I'll show that old witch what proper parkin is,' she yelled up to the roof, 'and when I get back, I'll show you the broomstick, useless husband!'

Hepzibah tumbled along the path in her drunken anger, losing first one shoe, then another, then – horrors! – the parkin itself. The precious round parkin bowled its way through the woods and towards the gully like a cartwheel. She cursed and stumbled after it down the slope, shouting and cawing like a murder of crows.

All the villagers came out to see what all the noise was about. They could see Billy's little cottage all lit up on one side of the gully, and then they saw the great round parkin rolling and bouncing down the way from the cottage, then they saw Hepzibah stumbling after it, trying to grab hold of it, losing her footing – and going right over the edge.

There at the bottom was the dragon, still hopeful, waiting with his jaws wide open. There was a great gollop that echoed around the place as the dragon swallowed Hepzibah whole.

'That were a bit grim to eat,' said the dragon, disappointed.

But the parkin wobbled and teetered on the top, then followed the same route as its maker had taken, over the edge. Now there was a great round parkin flying towards the dragon.

'Cor!' said the dragon. He opened his jaws wide, and then bit into the parkin so completely that his teeth got stuck.

Then the dragon couldn't talk any more.

That's when the folk of the village ran to get pitchforks and pickaxes and sledgehammers, but then they stopped. How could they get into the gully without getting burned?

The dragon sorted out that problem. He waddled out of the gully and down to the sea to wash off the treacly parkin from between his teeth, and stop them sticking together. They all followed, just in time to see the dragon fall in a huge bellyflop into the deep seawater, and stick his head down under the surface to wash it.

So the villagers ran to where the dragon was under the seawater. They beat and bashed and hit him with all the heavy tools they had, until he was out cold. Before the dragon could come round, the tide came in and drowned him.

The villagers looked at one another. 'What about Billy Biter?' and they ran up to Billy's cottage to check he was all right.

There was the door wide open, and the fire blazing merrily in the hearth, and the puss-cat washing itself in the corner. There was a nice, square bit of parkin on a baking sheet in front of the fire, and Billy Biter was mending the seat of his mother's chair. It was a scene of happiness and harmony and, from her own cottage over on the other side of the gully, I dare say that Mrs Greenaway could see it too.

That's how Filey Brigg was made, out of the bones and the body of that old dragon from the gully, his mouth all clogged with parkin, drowned in the sea and turned to stone. He still causes trouble for sailors, mind, but if you know where he is, you can do your best to avoid him.

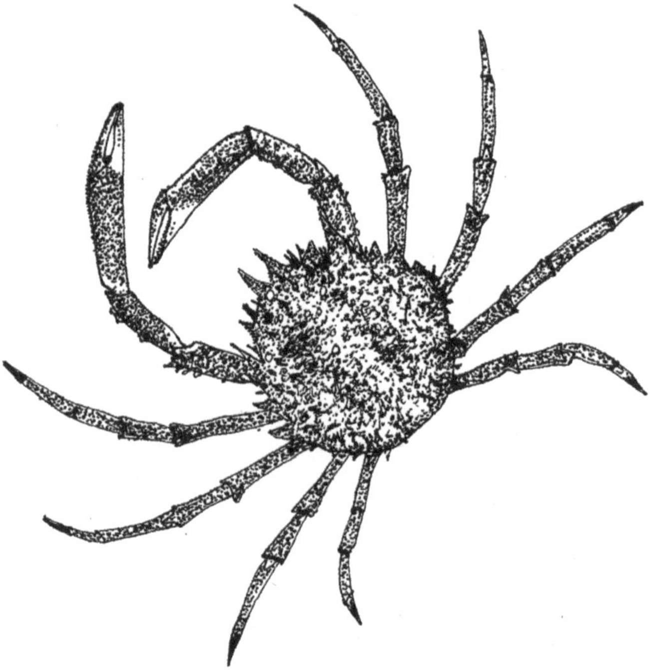

6

PIRATES AND PLUNDER

Merchant and pirate were for a long period one and the same person.

Friedrich Nietzsche (1844–1900)

On 18 January 2007, en route from Belgium to Portugal, the MSC *Napoli* was beached at Branscombe on the south-west coast of England after suffering severe damage in a storm off Lizard Point in Cornwall. A 5-mile oil spill caused serious problems for local sea birds, but that didn't make the news. Despite warnings from the police, over 200 people had arrived to scavenge from the *Napoli*'s containers that had washed ashore. Motorbikes, nappies, car parts, perfume and empty wine casks were all taken. A local cider maker even matured his cider in salvaged wine casks and later sold 'Shipwreck' cider brandy to London establishments at a premium.

For good or bad, the people around Lyme Bay were simply following in the footsteps of their ancestors. In the old days before aeroplanes and trains, everything brought into Britain was shipped from overseas. Without modern safety measures or navigation methods, shipwrecks were very common, particularly in the south-west of England due to its rocky shoreline and strong prevailing onshore winds. Other notorious areas included Goodwin Sands in the south-east, and on the Wirral in the north-west, but, in reality, unfortunate vessels could come to grief anywhere along the English coast.

For the local people living on the English coast, scavenging, plundering and benefiting from the sorry victims of these wrecks was a significant part of many livelihoods. Some might consider it unsavoury to scavenge from the misfortune of others; others might call it practical to take advantage of the opportunity.

Did people actively cause wrecks? There is no factual evidence of the practice of luring ships on to the rocks, but our folk tales have plenty to say about it. Some folklorists think that the wreckers themselves would spread stories about ghosts and murder, even cannibals, on the coast to deter people from getting too close to their business. But they would not have welcomed stories about the facts.

Scavenging becomes piracy when people actively choose to rob and plunder from other places of their choice, often with violence and murder thrown in. England's people have experienced piracy many times, particularly from Vikings and other invaders. They have also produced many pirates, including Samuel 'Black Sam' Bellamy and Edward 'Blackbeard' Teach. Most exploits of English pirates were overseas, driven by social change at home and facilitated by the expansion of merchant trading and slavery in the sixteenth, seventeenth and eighteenth centuries. For this book I have chosen folk tales of pirates who had a major impact on their home country of England, whether they enjoyed royal sponsorship or not.

THE WRECKER AND THE GHOST SHIP

This dramatic story has versions all along the Cornish and north Devon coast. It was originally recorded by William Bottrell in 1873, and speaks of the Tregaseal beach, not the nearby village of Tregeseal. The Hartland story of Copinger, the cruel Danish wrecker and pirate, has many similarities. The tale speaks quite effectively of the evil associated with wrecking, and the consequences for someone who chooses to make it a way of life.

Gales whipped up a frenzy around Cape Cornwall. The sky was nearly black in the middle of the day. Waves crashed into the rocks, and the wind was almost too strong to stand up in. Yet through the pelting rain, a small crowd of people were gathered outside a cottage set back from the sea at Tregaseal.

Inside the house, a man shouted and yelled in sheer terror, loud enough to be heard through the storm. 'Death be upon me! Ah! The pain! The pain of it!'

Yet nobody went in to help.

'Fetch the parson,' said one of the men to a young lad shivering at the back. 'The day has finally come.'

Some years before, on a very different kind of day when the sky was clear and the sunlight made the Atlantic shimmer, a curious ship rounded Cape Cornwall and made its way down towards Whitesands Bay, drifting towards Land's End.

The ship had a peculiar rig, which sent alarm all along the coast, because this was clearly a ship of pirates. A growing number of men, women and children watched the danger from behind the rocks, ready for trouble as the ship was nearing pistol range.

Then a small boat was lowered from the ship. Four men climbed down and waited with the oars, as another figure on the ship, manacled and chained, was forced down to join them. Everyone on the shore could see several pistols pointing at this man's head as he climbed clumsily over the side and down to the little boat. He was rowed to the shore, where the crew members (again with pistols) forced him to stand, then took off his chains.

Then, the prisoner attacked his captors in a frenzy of anger. But the four of them were too strong for one man, and easily overpowered him. They threw their prisoner in the shallow water, pushed off their boat from the shore, and left him standing in the sea and cursing them with such venom that some of the mothers put their hands over their children's' ears.

The ship now found its way out to sea, and nobody was sorry to see it go. But what about this poor man dumped on the shore? The good people of the village gave him food and drink and clothes, and waited to hear his story, but he would not tell. He was grumpy, which was understandable given his experience. But only time would tell the villagers what kind of man this was.

He didn't seem to want for money, and rented a small cottage near to Tregaseal. All was quiet, although the following winter there seemed to be a greater number of ships coming to grief on the rocks at Cape Cornwall.

Then slowly the truth came out. On dark winter nights, this fellow was out and about with his horse. He would fasten a lantern to the horse's neck, and take it up to the clifftop. Then he would hobble the horse by tying its head down to a foreleg, and drive it along the ground. From the sea, the swaying lantern would look exactly like the stern-light of a ship.

That lantern was more like the light of an angler fish attracting its prey. Other ships sailing by would expect plenty of room where another boat would be, and they came right in to shore, to be dashed on the rocks. That was when the man scrambled down to the shore to meet the wreckage. Any poor soul who was still alive from their disaster would meet no mercy from this man. He would knock them on the head with his hatchet, and cut off any hands that were grasping at the rocks. Once he was sure there was nobody left alive to give evidence against him, the man would take all the spoils from the wreck himself.

That's how this wicked wrecker made his living. Who knows how many hundreds of ships he lured on to the rocks, or how many innocent sailors lost their lives at his hands? He lived long, and became rich – but eventually, it happened.

One fine sunny day at harvest time, two men were scything a field a little below the wicked man's house. There wasn't a breath of wind to move the barley that day. But all at once, a strong gust of wind arrived, and in it the words were spoken: '*The time is come, but the man isn't come.*'

They looked out to sea, to where the wind had come from, and there, in Whitesands Bay, was a curious ship. It was black and heavy, square-rigged, with all her sails set, moving quite unnaturally against the wind and the tide. There was not a soul to be seen on board. Above the ship was a dark cloud, as if the ship carried its own personal storm along with it.

As the ship came under the cliff, so close that her masts could no longer be seen, the storm cloud rose high into the air and moved over the house of the wrecker at Tregaseal. The storm only raged there, over the cottage and over Cape Cornwall; elsewhere, the sunny, calm day persisted.

The two men left their work in terror, and as they walked they found neighbours crowding round the wrecker's cottage, none of them daring to go in, but one of them asking for the parson, for they all knew what kind of man was inside.

Finally, the parson, the doctor and a couple of stout-hearted fishermen went in. The wrecker was writhing on the floor. 'Ah! Ah! The Devil is clawing out my eyes with his fingernails! Death is come!'

They watched, ready to move if needed, and with every scream of pain the wrecker made, the room got darker and darker. Then, it suddenly became so bright that every hair on the wrecker's head could be clearly seen standing on end. Images of crashing waves and howling storms filled the room, and even the fishermen felt seasick.

The parson had begun his incantations. 'Be gone, Satan!' he cried, raising his hands, and channelling the Holy Spirit with all the power he could muster. 'You have no place in this community!'

The Devil did battle, but the parson was so strong that he reduced the evil spirit to the size of a hornet. Even he couldn't get rid of it completely, for there will always be evil in the world. There was a fearful crash of thunder from the storm clouds above the house, and a blaze of sheet lightning all around them. Every bit of furniture in that room burst into flame, and parson, doctor and fishermen all fled for their lives.

Outside, a violent storm was raging above the cottage and down to the rocks. The dark clouds writhed and seethed, turning in on themselves; then the clouds moved from Tregaseal over to the dark ship waiting off the shore. The ship moved out to sea together with its cloud, and many thankful eyes watched it disappear to the horizon.

It took a while before anyone was brave enough to go back into the cottage. They found the body of the old wrecker, a ghastly spectacle on the floor, his face mangled in terror.

The parson crossed himself. 'Prepare a coffin, so nobody need look on this face again.'

They got the body into a rough wooden coffin as quickly as they could, and four men lifted it. The coffin was much too light to contain a normal man's body.

'We'll not open it again,' said the parson. 'We need the safety of holy ground.'

As the bedraggled procession carried the coffin up to the church in the sunlight, one of the fishermen looked back to the cottage and the clifftop. Behind them at the back of the procession, a black pig was silently trotting along. It looked up at him with blood-red eyes.

'Hey!' he cried. 'Evil follows us!'

The procession stopped to look, but the black pig had disappeared.

When they all reached the stile of the churchyard, the dark cloud returned and settled over the whole place. 'To the church for safety!' cried the parson, and they all climbed hurriedly over the stile and ran into the church, leaving the coffin on the ground outside the holy sanctuary.

They were there for some time. A dark storm raged all night and howled around the church, while everyone inside huddled together for comfort.

At some point in the early morning, there was a great flash of light outside. The parson dared to look out of the door. A bolt of lightning had set fire to the coffin.

As the parson watched, the burning corpse of the wrecker, coffin and all, was whisked up into the dark sky and out of sight forever.

THE RAVENS AND THE WRECKER

Robert Stephen Hawker (1803–75) was, for most of his life, the vicar of Morwenstow, a small parish on the north coast of Cornwall. He had a reputation as a compassionate man who gave Christian burials to shipwrecked seamen, when formerly their bodies might have just been left in the sea. Before him, Morwenstow had been without a vicar for over a century. Hawker's little clifftop writing hut, made from driftwood, is now the smallest property in the National Trust's portfolio.

Hawker was quite a character, and he dressed flamboyantly – it was said that his socks were the only black things he ever wore. Besides dressing occasionally as a mermaid (see Chapter 1), excommunicating his cat for going mousing on Sundays, and keeping a pig as a pet, he invented the modern Church of England Harvest Festival. 'What a life mine would be if it were all written and published in a book,' he wrote. That's exactly what happened, with a book about Hawker published by Baring-Gould in 1876, and several other authors since.

This story was told to Parson Hawker by an old Morwenstow man, Tony Cleverdon. 'Wreck-candle' was apparently a particular kind of Neapolitan candle that wreckers would find on ships from the Mediterranean.

Some years ago, there was an old wrecker called Kinsman. When he couldn't get a wreck, he worked in the stone quarry.

One day he was halfway down the cliff face in the quarry when he saw two huge black ravens circling round his head. He couldn't very well duck, for fear of losing his balance, so he had to stay still. Those two ravens dropped two bits of wreck-candle at his feet.

'This means there's a wreck comin' in on the beach,' thought old Kinsman.

So he collected all his tools together and left them in the same spot to return to the following day, then went on his way to the wreck.

But there was no jetsam to be found anywhere, no matter how much he walked and scrambled and searched.

'Those ravens were tricking me,' he thought.

The next day, he went back to the quarry to work. But his tools were nowhere to be found, because the whole crag he had been working had given way. If he had stayed there on the previous day for even an hour longer, Kinsman would have been crushed to death.

Those ravens had known just how fond Kinsman was of wrecking. How crafty they had been, just to save his skin!

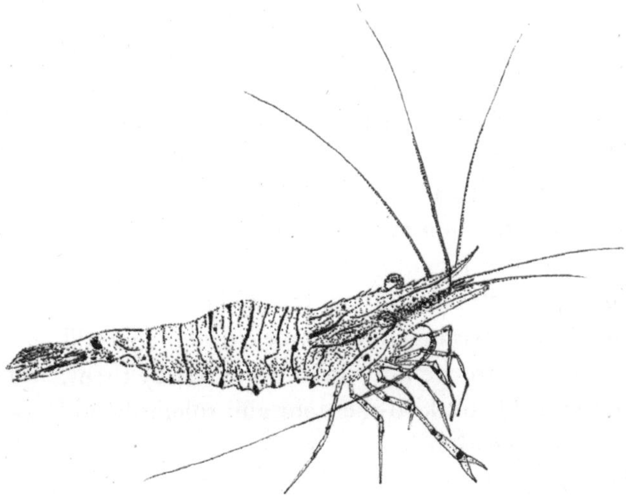

A Common Cause

Here's another tale of how all of the community got involved in a coastal opportunity – this time, a shipwreck. It comes from Walney Island off the Cumbrian coast, derived from Rollinson's 1997 Cumbrian Dictionary of Dialect, Tradition and Folklore. *This coastline is now transformed with offshore wind turbines, and it looks very different from the time of this story. There are similar tales from other parts of the English coast.*

It was Sunday, and everyone who was anyone on Walney Island was in church. The sermon was a long one, and there were many sighs and shuffles from the faithful congregation as the vicar launched into another holy aspect of his topic.

The church door opened and a lad's head peered in.

'There's a wreck!'

That was it. Bibles went flying, kneelers were discarded and the spiritual attention of the congregation was lost. There was a stampede for the door.

'Just a minute!' The vicar was waving his arms crossly and striding to the door, pushing through the crowd. 'Hold still.'

He made it to the door before the rest of them, and then turned with his back to the door and solemnly addressed his beloved congregation.

'There, now. Let's all of us have a fair start. Fair's fair,' said the vicar with a wink.

Then he was at the latch of the door and out of there, running down to the sea and the wreck, far ahead of the rest of them.

THE PIRATES OF LUNDY

In north Devon in the old days, it was really easy to get lost. There were no satnavs or phones, few maps and few real roads. Any journey could be perilous.

But what if you wanted to get lost in north Devon in the old days? That was more difficult. People didn't really venture very far from their communities, and so they made it their business to know everything about everyone else. Any changes, and any strangers, were noticed quickly.

What you needed was a place that was really difficult to get to … that didn't have any people living there … where you couldn't be watched and wouldn't be seen. A place that lots of people look at, but very few actually visit.

How about Lundy – the island of puffins? This tiny island has seen more than its fair share of skulduggery, some of it by people who really should have known better.

A lump of granite in the sea only 3 miles across and ⅝ of a mile wide, Lundy Island is a small island just off the north Devon coast. Ships have to navigate close to Lundy to avoid the fast-flowing currents of the Bristol Channel, and even in ancient times some of those boats have been full of people with less than honourable intentions.

In the eighth century, Lundy was used as a base for Viking invaders to the British Isles. The island belonged to the Knights Templar in the 1100s, still charged with the ancient duty of seeing off Scandinavian invaders.

In the thirteenth century, the de Marisco family of north Devon were notorious pirates, robbing ships of their valuable cargo and living very well from the proceeds. In 1235, an intruder tried to kill the king, Henry III, near Oxford. When captured, he said he had been employed by William de Marisco of Devon.

De Marisco was a wanted man. He fled to Lundy, where he built a stronghold and set himself up as king of Lundy. The king's men hunted him down, scaled the cliffs of Lundy and arrested de Marisco and sixteen of his 'subjects'. A storyteller of the time wrote: 'de Marisco was thrown into chains, condemned and sentenced to death. He was executed at the Tower, his body suspended in a sack, and when stiff in death, disembowelled, his bowels burnt, and his body divided into quarters.'

After this, Henry III had his own castle built on Lundy to make sure everyone knew it was his … but he should have guessed that it's very difficult to rule Lundy for long.

In the early 1500s, a gang of French pirates seized Lundy, only to be chased off by a brave band of Clovelly fishermen. In 1587, the authorities of Barnstaple raided Lundy again and made prisoners of the 'pirates and sea-rovers' that sheltered there, finding they wore 'great gold buttons, crimson taffeta and broad gold lace.' More mayhem continued into the 1600s and throughout the Civil War, with Lundy being occupied by Turkish, French, Spanish and homegrown English pirates at different times. All of them wanted Lundy for their own territory, a base from which to attack the wealthy merchant ships sailing from exotic places into Bristol.

But it was in the 1700s that the lawlessness of Lundy really passed into legend. Why? Because the most notorious Lundy pirate of them all was also the Member of Parliament for Barnstaple.

Thomas Benson was born in Bideford, the son of a wealthy merchant. In 1748, he leased Lundy Island, and in 1749 he was elected MP for Barnstaple. He also entered into a contract with the government for exporting convicts to the New World – that we now call North America. This was a lucrative trade at the time.

Benson's ships didn't get as far as America. He simply shipped the convicts to Lundy and kept them there, locking them up in the cave beneath de Marisco's old stronghold, together with any amount of smuggled and pirated goods such as wine, pewter, linen, salt and tobacco. Benson ruled Lundy like a king, and treated the poor prisoners as his slaves, but nobody suspected for years and years; after all, he *was* a Member of Parliament.

Not content with the riches he had, Thomas Benson then loaded a ship with fine goods and took out a hefty insurance policy before the boat left the dock. In the dark of night, the ship put down anchor at Lundy, its cargo was unloaded and the ship set sail again, soon to burn and sink. Benson went to cash in his policy.

Luckily, all the crew were rescued from the wreckage – but one of them confessed to the crime. Benson was rumbled, but he managed to escape to Portugal and was never brought to justice. And as for the convict slaves kept on the island? Happily, they broke out of the castle, took the longboat to Hartland, and were never seen again.

You might think these are tall tales from long ago. But the last man to declare himself king of Lundy, Martin Coles Harman, did so only a century ago, in 1924. He even had his own coins minted, with a puffin on one side and a picture of himself on the other. He wasn't sent to the Tower, but he was prosecuted and fined, nonetheless.

Lundy Island and the seas surrounding it are still a place to hide, and not just for humans. In 2010, Lundy became the centre of the UK's first Marine Conservation Zone – with a no-take zone in the sea to the east, meaning that all the fish and sea life under water can recover and flourish here now.

The lighthouses on Lundy signal to ships to keep away, although many people curious about this small island visit to see the rare birds blown off course from their migration routes, and of course to see the puffins.

But if you look in the island's caves, you will find the carvings made by generations of people who, centuries ago, ended up on Lundy hidden from the rest of the world – some who wanted to be there, and some who didn't.

Francis Drake the Magician

There must be a beginning of every matter, but the continuing unto the end yields the true glory. If we can thoroughly believe that this which we do is in defence of our religion and country, no doubt our merciful God for his Christ our Saviour's sake is able and will give us victory, though our sins be red.

Sir Francis Drake, from a letter to Sir Francis Walsingham, 1587 (modernised)

Sir Francis Drake was one of the first seafaring heroes of England, with a big personality to match. Born around 1540, he grew up to flourish as a pioneer of English seafaring and a political hot potato.

Francis Drake's story has endured through the centuries. The Spanish Armada must rate among England's top victories against invading forces; its warning beacons still mark the hills across south-west England. Drake still dances through England's school history books 'singeing the king of Spain's beard'. His quote above was published by The Times *on 20 November 1939, to inspire a country that found itself at war once again.*

There's no doubt that Drake achieved some amazing feats, ably assisted by fleets and their crews who worked hard to make a major sea campaign succeed in the sixteenth century. Between 1577 and 1589, Drake was the first Englishman to circumnavigate the globe in a single expedition, encountering new lands and many marvels and returning with precious treasure. He was second in command of the English national fleet at the time it defeated the Spanish Armada in 1588. At one point, Drake brought back more plundered gold for Queen Elizabeth than all the Crown's other income for an entire year – not to mention fabulous wealth for himself. Towards the end of his life, Drake was hailed as a national hero, knighted by the queen on his galleon The Golden Hind *and given his own coat of arms.*

Drake's achievements were all the more impressive given his lowly beginnings in life. He was the eldest of twelve, a Protestant vicar's son, who started his training as a ship's apprentice when he was very young. Following trading voyages along European coasts, he became tangled up with slave trade voyages to Africa and South America. Drake was involved in a battle with Spanish ships off the coast of Mexico, where he witnessed the genocide and cruelty of colonialism at first hand. He only just made it back to England, amid bitter accusations of betrayal by fellow captains. Following this, Drake renounced slavery, a principle he maintained for the rest of his life; he also vowed to attack the Spanish and plunder their colonial gold wherever he found it.

There are plenty of stories where Drake shows some respect for the welfare of others. He is recorded as sharing plunder fairly among crew members and leaving some for the vanquished. As mayor of Plymouth, he commissioned a wooden water channel, made of rot-resistant elm wood, to make sure the residents of this fine city could enjoy clean water from the moor above.

But with our modern sensibilities, it is difficult to learn of any details of Drake's exploits without calling him out for what he truly was – a pirate. His fabulous expeditions demanded courage, but also ruthlessness. Fuelled by Protestant zeal and personal grievance, Drake's voyages were sponsored by many rich people investing in his plundering. They included Queen Elizabeth herself, although the queen was canny enough not to announce the fact when involved in foreign policy discussions to do with Spain.

Many people died in Drake's fleets, or died as a result of his theft and pillage, and died in the wars with the Spanish that he helped to provoke. Drake's particular brand of cocksure, state-sponsored piracy was a catalyst for the beginnings of the British Empire, with all the atrocities that followed.

To Drake's countrymen in sixteenth-century Devon, however, the accomplishments of this extraordinary man must have seemed close to wizardry. People said that Drake had a magic scrying mirror, similar to the obsidian mirror used by the contemporary mystic John Dee. In that mirror, Drake was said to be able to see all the ships in the world. Now that all of us carry a scrying glass in our pockets (or as we call it, a mobile phone) this might seem underwhelming, but back in the day it was a story of a powerful man who achieved impossible things … in other words, a magician. Anna Bray, who recorded some local Devon tales of Drake in 1844, noted: 'All the stories told of him are of a wild and extravagant nature.'

The legends that have arisen about Drake are a good example of how folk tales can arise from extraordinary characters and notable events, and they do embroider some truths. Although the story of Drake playing bowls on Plymouth Hoe may have been invented shortly after the Armada, it's true that Drake's fire-ships played a large part in the English victory against the Spanish, on that occasion at least. Drake's second wife was indeed Elizabeth Sydenham, and the cannon ball in the story still exists (it's said to be a meteorite). Drake's Drum, or at least its carefully crafted replica, can be seen in the Box Museum at Plymouth today; two British army officers claimed they heard the drum beating during the Battle of Britain in 1940. Drake's home, Buckland Abbey, now owned by the National Trust, is a fabulous place to visit.

Sir Francis Drake, doughty Devonian and vice admiral of the English Navy, had power over land and air and water. The Spanish called him 'El Draco', 'the dragon'. The gold he plundered from them made little difference to the Spanish king, but it meant a fortune to England. Drake knew that he could defeat the Spanish any time he wanted, keeping England and her people safe.

Spain was, at that time, one of the most powerful countries on Earth, proudly Catholic and dominating Europe and its colonies. Philip II of Spain had married Mary Tudor, who tried to return England to the Catholic faith, but she had died without children, and her sister, Elizabeth, had not only refused Philip's hand in marriage, she was also determinedly Protestant.

England at that time was an insignificant country, but to Philip it was an annoyance, and it became even more of a problem when Francis Drake got to work. Stealing gold from the Spanish colonies in the New World, and even taking their ships, Drake taunted the Spanish again and again until Philip had had enough. He would invade England and return this heathen country to the true faith.

The Spanish Armada that Philip assembled was the most powerful war fleet that Europe had ever known, with 130 ships, 8,000 sailors, 18,000 soldiers and 2,500 guns. The king of Spain meant business; he meant to take England for his own, and the country was just as scared as when the Normans had invaded 500 years earlier. Fear swept the nation.

On 29 July 1588, the Armada was sighted from the Lizard in Cornwall. and the beacons were lit all the way across England to warn of the impending invasion. Word was sent to Francis Drake in Plymouth, the vice admiral of the fleet, to ready himself and his fleet for war.

Drake at that time was playing a game of bowls with his friends on Plymouth Hoe.

'There's no hurry,' he said as he picked up another bowling ball and bowled it down the green. 'There's plenty of time to finish our game. The Spanish can wait.'

The game of bowls was agonisingly slow, in the middle of a town frantic with fear.

Drake's men were hopping up and down with nervous energy. Finally, the game was done. 'Time to go!' they cried, and tried to hurry Drake from the games green.

But Drake had other ideas. He went from Plymouth Hoe to Devil's Point, a good point on the coast to look out to Plymouth Sound and the open sea.

Drake sat down and got out his sailor's knife, and found an old chunk of wood, and started to whittle. Every sliver of wood that he whittled away floated up into the sea breeze and down into Plymouth Sound, where it became a fine ship. Soon there was a whole fleet of galleons ready to beat the Spanish Armada.

The sails of Drake's ships billowed in the wind, each weighed down with a cargo of gunpowder. Each ship sparkled with magic and burst into flame. Each one became a fire-ship.

Sailing in amongst the Spanish galleons, they started the whole defeat of the mighty Spanish Armada – helped along by the sea winds and the fire magic of Francis Drake.

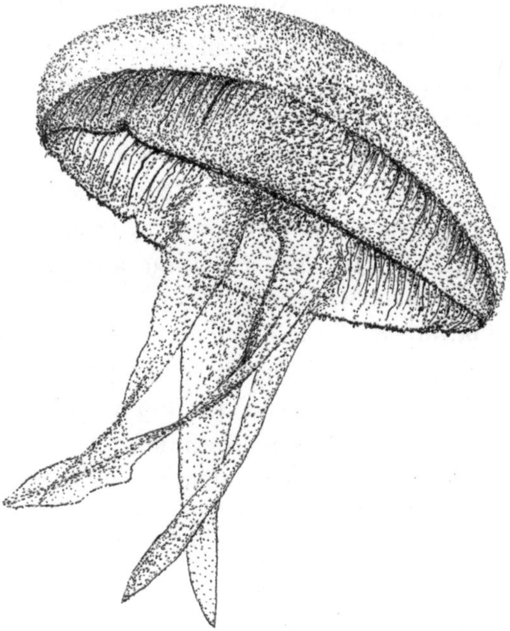

Elizabeth Sydenham was rich and Elizabeth Sydenham was beautiful. Daughter of the High Sheriff of Somerset, heiress of a country estate … she could have any man in the country she wanted. But the very one she chose was the one her father didn't want her to marry. His name was Francis Drake.

'Why won't you consider John Wyndham?' cried her father. 'He is a much better match – he is richer, taller, less of the Devonshire burr, more presentable in court. Let's face it my dear, Drake is not marriageable material. He's nothing more than a pirate!'

But Elizabeth would have none of it. 'I want Francis Drake, and I will marry Francis Drake. I have pledged myself to him. There will be no other for me. When he comes back from Africa, we will be married Father, and you will see me happy.'

Elizabeth was telling a bit of a fib, there. She knew what few others in the kingdom knew, apart from the queen herself: Drake was not just going to Africa. Drake had a mad plan. Drake was determined to be the first Englishman to travel around the globe.

'I will bring back such treasure for you, my love, we will marry and be happy,' he had said. 'Just wait a year or two, and our fortunes will be made, God willing.'

You would be forgiven for thinking that Drake wanted to have the best of both worlds, to be married and to be free for adventure. But Elizabeth was smitten, and she readily agreed to wait for Drake, and to keep his secret in the meantime.

The time dragged. The first six months were tough enough, but by the time a year of waiting had gone by, and there was only scant news from Drake, Elizabeth's father could wait no longer. 'Drake will perish on the high seas,' he said. 'Whoever heard of a man choosing the chaos of the ocean above the woman he loves? I tell you, Wyndham is a much better match for you, and he will wait, with his land, and his assurance of security with no adventure at all. Marry Wyndham, Elizabeth, and forget your pirate.'

Elizabeth refused. 'I will wait for Drake to return. He will return, I know it,' she said.

Another year went by, Wyndham was patient, but Elizabeth's father was more persistent. 'Do you wish for your best years to go by, waiting for a pirate? Marry John, I insist on it.'

Elizabeth refused. 'Drake will return yet,' she said.

After the third year, Elizabeth was worried. Drake had never been away for such a long time, and any news of him has been months before. She willed him to still be alive, but life was short in those days, and her father eventually persuaded Elizabeth that the best route was to marry John Wyndham.

The wedding day at Stogumber church was overcast, but Elizabeth made the best of it. Her wedding gown swished on the tiles of the church as she walked towards Wyndham, and now she was standing in front of the vicar with this other man, and still all she could think about was Drake.

At that crucial moment, a loud CRACK! sounded above them. The wooden church roof splintered and a cannonball hit the ground at speed, out of nowhere. It thudded into the floor between the bride and the groom and stole the show, with people running in all directions.

Elizabeth, covered in splinters and dust, walked back towards the altar and peered at the cannonball.

'This is a sign,' she said. 'Drake will return soon. I will marry him, I will not marry another.'

Three days later, in the calm after the calamity and the arguments, Elizabeth was walking in nearby Taunton when a beggar man in the gutter caught her eye. 'Got a gold piece to spare?' He looked up at her and flashed a wide grin. Elizabeth gasped, and fell into the arms of her beloved Francis Drake. He may have been disguised as a beggar, but he had brought back more gold and silver plunder than newlyweds would ever need.

Elizabeth and Francis were married, and if her father didn't like it, he knew his daughter too well by now to protest any more.

Devon people know that when England is in mortal danger, Francis Drake will return. They say that Drake has already returned from the dead, incarnated again as our other great sea heroes, and that he will come back again yet. He'll be heralded by the beating of his old drum, playing all by itself.

7

THE HUNGRY SEA

Full fathom five thy father lies;
Of his bones are coral made;
Those are pearls that were his eyes:
Nothing of him that doth fade,
But doth suffer a sea-change
Into something rich and strange.
Sea-nymphs hourly ring his knell:
Ding-dong.
Hark! now I hear them, — ding-dong, bell.

William Shakespeare (1564–1616) from The Tempest,
Act 1 Scene 2

It takes a particular kind of courage to work with the gods of the sea, for many reasons. You could easily lose your life. When you are on a boat, with all the deep ocean beneath, you're at the mercy of the skills of whoever is sailing the vessel you happen to be on, and also at the mercy of the elements.

No wonder that fate and luck are taken so seriously by those who make their living on the waves. Here are stories of superstitions, ghosts and signs of doom that will make you shiver.

A Gaggle of Ghosts

Next time you are on the English coast or sailing the seas, blink and you might just catch a dark memory flitting by. Our coasts are full of ghosts. Some of them relate to the many tragedies that have occurred down the centuries. Others warn of tragedy to come, or perhaps try to avoid it.

Many of these folk tales are very short – and I think this makes them more authentic. When you have seen a ghostly apparition, that itself is the main story. What else is there to do but wonder at it?

England's coasts abound with ghost ships, appearing where their wreckage originally occurred, and sometimes even sailing on to dry land before disappearing.

At Goodwin Sands, the famous 'ship-eater' sandbank off the coast of Kent, which has laid claim to over 2,000 ships in its time, many different ghost ships have become muddled in their origins and stories over the years. Other ghost ships might appear as premonitions of other disasters, or to mark the anniversary of evil deeds that led to their wrecking.

This little story comes from the Cornish coast, recorded in the late nineteenth century. A 'hobbler' was a rowing boat that helped either to guide larger ships into port, or to help offload goods from larger ships into smaller ports. The competition was often intense between local crews, who would race to be the first to reach a ship. 'Hooking' the ship meant throwing a boat hook over the side, winning yourselves the right to help that ship (and earn money from it). It could be a dangerous pursuit in difficult conditions, particularly as most sailors couldn't swim. This hobbler got more than it bargained for.

One night, a gig's crew was called to a hobble to the west of St Ives Head. Several boats put off from the shore and the chase was on. All of them were desperate to be the first to the great ship, which looked like a foreign one with a light over her bows.

The first boat to launch was well ahead of the others. The men's rowing was skilled and strong. They were so close now, they could see the sailors on deck of the ship. The helmsman cried out, 'Stand ready to board!' The sailor rowing the bow oar slipped it out of its lock and stood forward, ready to spring aboard the ship.

The man standing leant forward to grasp the ship's bulwark, but his hand grasped at … nothing at all. He lost his balance and would have gone in the sea, but for a quick-thinking man behind him who pulled him backwards.

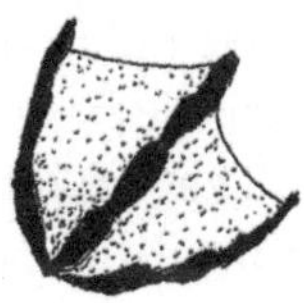

Then the ship and the lights disappeared.

All the men rowed back to St Ives, wondering at the ghost ship.

The following morning, the ship *Neptune*, sailing from London, was wrecked at Gwithian, and all souls on board perished.

Peel Castle on the Isle of Man has some great stories, including a giant who is said to be Manannan, the god of the sea himself. Another is a ghost dog called the Mauthe Doog. Something akin to a black, curly-haired spaniel, this is apparently very bad tempered and can drive a man mad, although (more helpfully) it does bark when a storm is on its way.

The Mauthe Doog is one example of ghostly dog apparitions all over the country, sometimes called Black Shuck or simply Black Dog.

'Where's the skipper, then?'

The crew of the fishing boat were waiting that evening for a night's fishing. They had been waiting for a good two hours and still the skipper hadn't turned up.

He didn't turn up. They all went home, wondering what had happened.

They found the skipper the next morning, indoors and already at his drink because the weather was atrocious. Here's what he told them.

'I was walking down the road from the top of the town,' he said, 'when a huge black dog blocked my path. Massive it was, and it went for me as if it had been waiting!'

'I went back home and I got a big stick. There was the black dog again, waiting for me in the same place; that stick made no difference to him. He would not let me past, no matter which way I tried to go.'

'In the end, I decided it was a sign, and so I went home again. And this morning, a huge gale whipped up out of nowhere – it would have killed the lot of us on that boat. I think it was the Mauthe Doog, and I think it knew.'

The shops in Whitby are well known to be full of spirits, and that's not just liquor for the fishermen.

A man from Guisborough walked into a Whitby shop, but the shopkeeper wasn't waiting for him there. Instead, waiting about, right in front of him, was a mirror image of himself, but it was all wispy and grey-looking. It was his waff, or his wraith.

The waff wasn't a welcome sight at all. The man knew that it was pure bad luck to see it, and that it would mean his death soon enough.

There was only one way to avoid it, and that was to be bold.

He walked right up to the waff. 'What's thou doing here?' he demanded, loudly and sternly, as if he was shooing a cow out of the shop. 'Get out. GET OUT! Get thy ways, yom, I say; get thy ways yom.'

The waff's eyebrow went up, its lower lip stuck out, and it looked crestfallen. It slunk out of the shop and down the road, and with it the waff took all the man's bad luck.

Crimdon Dene beach, north of Hartlepool, was once a favourite holiday spot for mining families. It's still a beautiful beach and a holiday park haunt. This story, recorded by the Rev. Forbes Phillips (writing as Athol Forbes) in his 1909 book The Romance of Smuggling, *is great fun.*

Sometime in the mid-1800s, a coastguard called Murray was walking towards Crimdon Dene beach one moonlight evening on his nightly patrol when he spied two figures on shore signalling to a small boat at sea.

He could see clearly that one of the men was Matthew Horsley, well known to him as a local smuggler. The boat, with about six men on it, was obviously carrying contraband.

Murray was outnumbered and he would be stupid to tackle them. But he couldn't let them get away. What should he do?

He quietly knocked on the door of a nearby cottage, and asked to borrow a white sheet. Murray draped himself in this and then waded out to sea from behind some rocks. Whatever was in the boat was being unloaded. He was all set to go.

One of the men in the boat saw the apparition, screamed, jumped in the water and waded to shore. Murray took his chance and began to wail as hauntingly as he could. 'Horsley! Horsley! Matthew … Horsley!'

All the smugglers saw was a pale shape rising from the water, lit by the moon over the sea. They ran for their lives.

The little boat was left behind. It was full of contraband tobacco. Murray marked all the packages and then waited with the boat for the next duty coastguard to start his shift.

Murray forgot to take off the sheet – or did he quite enjoy wearing it? When he finally turned up, the next coastguardsman saw a bedraggled ghost guarding a little boat, dutifully carrying out the orders of Her Majesty's Customs.

For Whom the Bell Tolls

Bells in our coastal folk tales are often associated with doom, death or warning. If the folk tales are to be believed, most of the coast of England is serenaded with doomed underwater bells on a regular basis.

Some of these tales might come from the turbulent religious changes of the sixteenth century, when the establishment of the Protestant Church of England led to a number of church bells being removed and shipped overseas, often to the horror of local parishioners who considered it bad luck.

A ship's own bell is usually exempt from such superstitions of doom. But if you are on a ship in a storm and the ship's bell rings of its own accord, then be very worried indeed.

This story was collected in Herefordshire in the 1890s, but strangely there is no place called Kentsham in this land-locked county. Withies (willows) were used to make ropes that were very strong under tension, although the withies in this story must have been quite substantial!

Once there was a famous bell foundry abroad, and the people of England who enjoyed the sounds of bells from this foundry considered themselves blessed indeed. Although it was expensive to procure one of these fine bells, a competition arose between parishes about who could have the finest bell from this particular foundry.

All the bells were called Great Tom, and so Great Tom of York, and Great Tom of Lincoln and Great Tom of Christchurch were all made, shipped to England on the same dutiful boat, and brought with great challenge and jubilation to their places of rest, where their peals delighted congregations.

Now it was the turn of Kentsham, who had ordered the biggest and the greatest and heaviest Great Tom of all.

There was some anxiety as Kentsham Great Tom drew near to the shore. Great winches and many men crowded around to lift it from the boat. Heave! Little by little, the bell was raised up on stout ropes and moved on planks and rollers towards the shore.

The captain was beside himself with excitement. At one point he swore out loud and, with that, the main rope snapped in two. Great Tom fell, slipped against the side of the boat and disappeared out of sight into the sea.

The captain didn't have any drinks bought for him that night, and there was no celebration. Instead the local people called for the cunning man and asked him what they should do.

'Take six milk-white cows which have never seen the yoke,' said the cunning man, 'and use withy bands that have never been used before, and don't let any man or woman utter a single word until the bell gets to the top of the hill.'

So the withies were cut and twined together to make great strong ropes, and they were bound to the bell in the shallow salt water and bound to six milk-white cows. They pulled and struggled and pulled, and at last the great bell emerged from the sea, bound in its withies, and made its way slowly up the hill towards the church. Only the bellows of the cows and the drag of the bell on the ground could be heard. All the people were silent, as they had been instructed.

The progress was slow, and the tension in the air was huge. Would the withies hold? But now the bell was nearly, nearly at the top of the hill, on a ledge before the final summit. The captain of the boat was so happy he couldn't help himself.

'In spite of all the devils in Hell, we've brought to land the Kentsham Bell!' he cried.

But the bell wasn't quite there yet. As soon as the captain spoke, the withies snapped and the bell rumbled and rolled its way back down the hill, clanging all the way. It had gathered some pace by the bottom of the hill and the clanging stopped as Great Tom plunged into the depths of the ocean, further out this time, into the deeps.

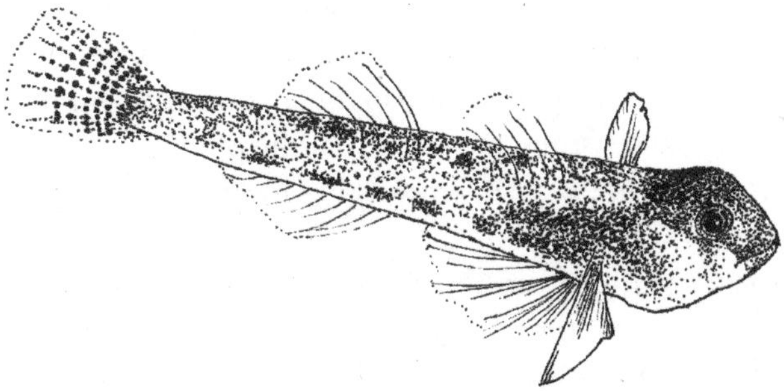

Nobody has ever set eyes on the bell since that day. Some say that it clangs and tolls beneath the waves. If you can find Kentsham, perhaps you will hear it too.

The old parish of Forrabury includes Boscastle and the area around. This part of north Cornwall is famous for its rivalry between Boscastle and nearby Tintagel; here is one of the reasons why.

Tintagel church had fine bells which are said to have rung peals of joy at the marriage of Arthur, and to have tolled solemnly at his death.

Forrabury wanted even better bells than that for their church.

The new bells were ordered from Spain, and cast, and blessed, and brought to Forrabury by sea. Of course the weather was fair for the event, and the boat moved serenely along the north Cornwall coast towards the entrance to Boscastle harbour.

The peal of Tintagel's church bells could be clearly heard by the crew of the boat. When the pilot heard the blessed sound, he crossed himself devoutly and bent his knee.

The captain laughed at him. 'It's skill that gives us a safe voyage, lad, skill, nothing to do with being nailed on a cross.'

The pilot was horrified. 'How could you say that, a good Christian man?' But this goaded the captain to utter more and more profanities, laughing and laughing at the sky and the waves and the ragged coastline, but mostly at the pilot.

'May God bless you anyway!' said the pilot. 'May he forgive you!'

Those watching from the cliffs saw the huge wave swelling from far the ocean, travelling at pace towards that boat. The ship did not rise upon it, of course, but it was overcome, and sank immediately, only a few hundred yards from Boscastle.

As the boat went down, the muffled sound of bells could be heard, as if ringing a death knell for everyone on board. They say that only the good pilot managed to escape with his life. The church tower in Forrabury remained silent.

When a storm is coming and there is a threat from the sea, the bells of Forrabury can be heard clearly from the sea, and everyone in both Boscastle and Tintagel knows exactly what it means.

This little Norfolk story was collected by Ruth Tongue's uncle in the early twentieth century. It reminds me of the emotions behind the story of Dunwich in Suffolk (chapter 8).

In the old days, there was a village on the Norfolk coast where the bells were rung during bad weather to warn the ships off the quicksands.

This angered the gods of the sea: they were denied their victims. So the sea worked and worked to erode the cliffs on which that little church stood, and it claimed more and more of the land as it went.

Soon, all the people of the village had retreated and built new houses at a safe distance from the coast, and only the church was left teetering on a crumbling cliff, overlooking the waves.

The old priest from the village still walked up to the cliff and rang the church bells on stormy nights. He considered it his duty to warn people of the danger, although as he got older and the cliff got crumblier, he suspected the sea would claim him in the end.

One night there was a great storm. A ship was seen out to sea, and the old boy set out in pelting rain and howling winds towards the church to warn it off. As he got close to the church, the path itself crumbled beneath his feet, and he had to crawl along a section of it for fear of losing his balance on the cliff.

He finally made it to the bell tower, and as he got hold of the bell ropes and began to ring the bells, a church window crashed inwards with the power of a high wave. The sea was too close, and the sea-gods had their prey now. As he rang and rang the bell and the sound cut through the storm, the church itself crumbled around the old priest; then the bell tower itself collapsed. The cliff, and the church it was standing on, slid down into the sea, carrying the old man along too.

The following morning, the storm was done and the ship was still lying a safe distance from the shore. The villagers came out to find the cliff and the church had gone, and they mourned the old priest.

But the bells continued to ring, from under the waves. They still toll even today, whenever the weather is bad, because the faithful priest is still trying to save lives from under the North Sea.

Unlucky for Some

Working with the sea is a matter of life or death, on a daily basis. That's probably the reason why there seem to be more superstitions in the folklore of the sea than in any part of the land of England.

If you are building a boat, don't start on a Friday, and make sure that you include some ash or rowan in the wood to help ward off evil spirits. Don't launch it on a Friday either. Seeing a clergyman on your way to launching the boat is bad luck.

When you get on the boat, on no account bring a woman with you, because they are bad luck on board. Don't bring flowers either, you aren't going to a funeral. Don't clap or whistle when you're on board, because that will bring thunder and gales. If you see a rat leaving the ship, you should also leave it immediately – that is a very bad omen.

I wonder how any folk tales about the sea ever actually came to be passed on, because it was considered unlucky to tell them. In fact, I wonder whether the ghost of some eighteenth-century sailor is watching me write these words and tutting, 'A woman writing these tales … you'll do us sailors nothing but harm.' I would tell him, of course, that the world doesn't work like that these days and, also, through hearing these stories, we are all keeping his memory and spirit alive. Perhaps, just to be sure, after you've read this chapter you might want to whisper a little prayer for the safety of all those working on the sea.

My first sad little story about superstition comes from North Yorkshire. In this case, the bad luck doesn't come from actual spinning, the offence is in the winding of the wool. I wonder if it's a premonition of disaster, or the actual cause of it?

The second story comes from Great Yarmouth in Norfolk, concerning a difficult subject for sailors: Friday. Apparently this was unlucky because it was the day of the Crucifixion, so it meant death. Eagle-eyed folklorists might also notice that it's the day before the weekend, and who wants to be out at sea on the weekend?

A young fisherman travelled inland to visit his relatives. During his visit, he met a young woman he really liked, and soon the two of them were married.

He brought her back to live in his little fishing village, so that he could go out on the boats and she would have a community around her. Although his new wife was a good woman, she was strange to the coast and the ways of the sea. She often laughed at the sayings of the fishermen's wives and the strange superstitions that everyone followed.

One night, when her husband was away on a long fishing trip, one of the young woman's new friends – the wife of another fisherman – called by for a cup of tea and a chat. She found the young woman spinning by the hearth, and just about to wind the spun wool into a ball.

She ran forward in horror. 'Stop, stop! That's such bad luck while your husband is away!'

'Don't be daft,' said the newcomer. 'Can't I even wind a bit of wool for fear of what might happen to me?'

'It's not about you,' said the local woman. 'Don't you know what might happen? Don't tempt fate!'

She was getting nowhere, and so she went to get help. Soon there was a whole crowd of fishermen's wives in the little cottage, all begging the newcomer to stop her spinning – and on no account to start winding her wool.

'Put the work down!'

'It's just not worth it!'

'Think of your husband!'

The more they protested and pleaded, the more the new wife was determined. 'Look,' she said, taking the end of the spun wool from the bobbin, 'look, nothing bad is happening here, as I … ' (at this she took and end of the wool began to wind it around her elbow and her hand) … 'start to wind it around, and then around.'

She turned round with a grin, but all the other women had fled shrieking from the room.

'Funny old lot,' she said, and carried on winding her wool. It slipped from her hands three times that evening, but she picked it up and carried on until she was finished.

The next morning, the newcomer bumped into one of the other fishermen's wives in the village. They asked her if she had completed her work the evening before.

'I wound all my wool, and no harm has come of it, look!' She turned around in the street, smiling.

'Did the wool slip from your hands at all?' asked the fisherman's wife anxiously.

'Not much. Only two or three times, I'd say, because I know what I'm doing. Yes, three times I'd have dropped it. What's the matter?'

The fisherman's wife had gone pale.

'It's a bad omen,' she said, and walked away shaking her head.

When her husband returned from his fishing trip, he heard the story of the winding of the wool. He was horrified. He had grown up with all the old stories too, and he understood exactly what it meant.

'It's very clear,' he said, head in hands. 'If the wool has slipped out of your hands three times, then it means I will return safely twice more, but the third time I will not return from the sea – it will take my life.'

'Don't be daft,' said his wife.

'Why take the risk? Why didn't you listen?' cried her husband. 'I'm back safe this time – and the next time I go out on the sea will have to be my last time. I'm not risking another fishing trip after that.'

He came back safe from his next fishing trip, sure enough. By then the young couple had other plans; they set up a little shop together in the village, and all was well with both of them. He didn't have to go out to sea again.

Four years later there was a great storm on the coast, catching many boats unawares. Late that evening, the lifeboat went out from the village, and all the able men who could volunteer were called out to help. The young village shopkeeper was one of them, and he went out in the storm on the lifeboat.

An hour or so later, he was just dragging the last survivor from a wreck into the lifeboat, when a huge wave washed over the side of the boat and swept him into the sea.

His body was washed up on the shore the next morning.

Now all the fishermen's wives of the village did their best to comfort the young shopkeeper's widow, the newcomer. They supported her as her husband was buried, and helped her get through the difficult days afterwards.

But one day soon after, the young woman packed up the shop and fled the village for good. She couldn't bear the grief and the guilt of what she might have done to her husband, all those years before when she had been winding wool.

She never showed her face there again.

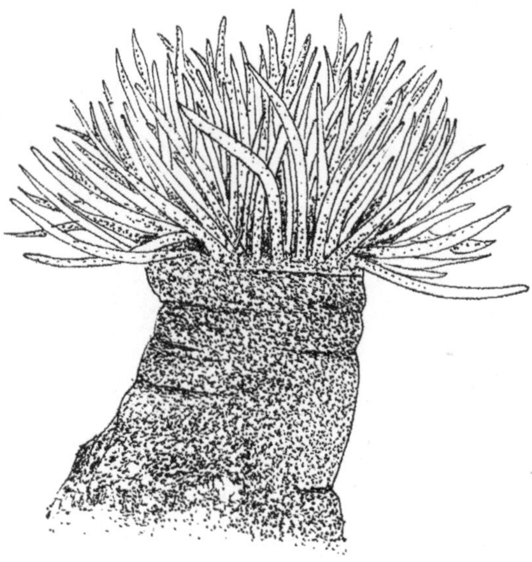

Many moons and many years ago, there was a man living at Yarmouth called Friday. He built himself a lugger, and he had it finished on a Friday.

The day he launched and christened the boat was a Friday, so he called it the good ship *Friday*.

When everything was ready, the boat was taken out of harbour on a Friday by her skipper, who (by way of being related to the original man Friday whose boat it was) was also called Friday.

Anything of any note that happened to, or in, or on that boat was on a Friday. It was out on the sea longer than expected …

But the boat came back in one Friday morning, carrying one of the largest takes of herring anyone in Yarmouth had ever seen.

That was some luck!

The boat went out again the following Friday and got a load of fish, nearly as good a catch as the last time. It also picked up two big old anchors and cables, and a derelict collier, and a billy-boy schooner too.

The third time the Friday boat went out …

It hasn't come back yet.

THE OMENS OF BIRDS

Bird migrations are sometimes called 'the herring spear' by fishermen, as the sound of flocks of birds is meant to presage a good catch of herring. Other birds calling in the night have a more malevolent reputation.

It has always been unlucky to kill sea birds, even before the famous albatross in Samuel Taylor Coleridge's The Rime of the Ancient Mariner. *Sailors think they are a sign of rough weather, and (often rightly) assume birds might be a sign of good fishing to be had. Some traditions say that the souls of dead sailors move into gulls. Human souls are also carried by other birds, including ravens, petrels, gannets and choughs.*

I'm a big fan of choughs. These artful, cliff-dwelling members of the crow family have bright red bills and an otherworldly 'peow-peow' call. Happily, choughs are making a comeback on the Cornish coast and elsewhere in the British Isles. They also have claim to a very special soul from the folklore world.

King Arthur was the greatest king that Britain has ever known. He was born next to the sea at Tintagel Castle, to his mother the Lady Igraine and his father Uther Pendragon, but he was whisked away from the coast by Merlin.

Arthur also met his end at the sea, after he was mortally wounded in battle. Faithful Bedivere gave Excalibur back to the Lady of the Lake, and some say that Arthur was then brought back to Cornwall's sacred coast and carried away over the ocean, into the mist of the Atlantic. When Britain is in trouble, when its people are in their time of greatest need, they say that Arthur will come to our aid again, together with his Knights of the Round Table.

But some other people say that Arthur never died on that boat. They say he simply transformed into a chough, and that's how he guards the people of these islands.

When he is needed, he will change back into his human form and come to help us. I don't know what sea birds the Knights of the Round Table are, but I can take a guess at Lancelot, can't you?

If you see a chough, it's important that you greet him in the proper manner. Make sure you bow, or curtsey, and say, 'Good afternoon, Your Highness.'

It's the proper way to address our once and future king.

8

BATTLING THE TIDE

No man is an island, entire of itself.

John Donne (1571–1631)

The past is not dead, it is living in us, and will be alive in the future, which we are now helping to make.

William Morris (1834–96)

On 1 December 1990, Englishman Graham Fagg and Frenchman Philippe Cozette shook hands under the English Channel, and we were no longer an island. The Channel Tunnel had broken through. People joked that it was the first time someone had travelled overland from England to France for 8,000 years.

In truth, our transport systems hadn't relied on the sea for much of the twentieth century. The advent of flight, and our ever-developing communications systems, mean that as a human race we are now more connected, and less island-like, than ever. As modern life has sped up, society's treatment of our coasts and seas has changed.

England's contemporary relationship with the sea is full of challenges. But all seas are, of course, connected. The dynamics of the English marine environment are changing more rapidly than we have ever known. As we realise the impact of human life and carbon emissions on the Earth's systems, the oceans are already warming and sea levels are rising. If the world continues towards a high emissions scenario, latest models predict that by the end of the century, UK seas will be 3°C warmer, seawater will be more acidic, and sea level could rise by up to 80cm. Climate change will mean more violent and extreme weather for the vulnerable little islands of Britain. Coastal erosion will increase and even major cities could flood.

Here are some folk tale responses to change on our coasts and in our seas. Some of them speak of action through community, betrayal or courage. Others simply tell of magic and acts of nature beyond our ability to control.

Each one of these tales offers some food for thought on the future of England's coasts and seas. Whether in Anglo-Saxon, Tudor or Victorian times, post-Brexit England, or ahead in the twenty-first century, the ocean remains a major part of our nation's life. Salt water defines us, it surrounds us, it defies control and definition – and sometimes it brooks no argument.

King Canute

This story has become an English turn of phrase. Even today, if somebody is called 'Canute' it means that they are arrogant and think they can control affairs outside the power of humans, even the powers of the tide itself. But that's not the message of the original story.

The power of monarchy holds some interesting nuance in our folk tales. In traditional stories all over the world, kings and queens are expected to hold stewardship and sovereignty over the land and sea. However, there is a clear tension between the power asserted by a king, and the power held by the Christian God. In a secular sense, you could call this mortal power versus the power of nature.

The story of Canute and the tide shows this power struggle. Some interpret the story as Canute asserting his absolute dominion over the waves. Others choose to focus on Canute's apparent humility in showing that only God has the power to move the waves. It's an interesting admission of mortality, given the widespread and pervasive belief in English folklore that kings couldn't drown.

The Danish prince Canute, or Cnut, was king of England from 1016 to 1035, following years of battles between the Vikings and the Anglo-Saxons that had brought England to its knees. Canute eventually ruled over most of England's people, including Mercians and West Saxons. He was considered successful as he brought an uneasy peace to England for two decades, subsequently winning the kingships of both Denmark and Norway and attempting to bring all their people together into one culture. It's fair to say that Canute was an ambitious man, and far from benign. He seemed to fully understand the power that the Church held over his people, and was apparently a devout Christian himself, despite insisting on taking two wives at the same time.

The story of how Canute tried to command the waves was recorded by Henry of Huntingdon in the twelfth century. Several places claim to be the actual spot on the coast where the story happened, including Thorney Island (now Westminster), Bosham in Sussex, Southampton,

Wallasey on the north coast of the Wirral, and at Gainsborough in Lincolnshire where Canute apparently tried to stop a tidal bore on the River Trent.

Everywhere King Canute went, the court went with him. Fawning courtiers fell over themselves to do his bidding and gain his favour. Ambitious young men constantly presented the king with ideas and flattery and assurances of his power.

One day, the king had had enough of it.

The court was travelling near the coast, and so he ordered that his throne should be taken and put on the beach, down on the sand near to where the salt water was lapping.

King Canute went to sit on the throne and look out over the waves. Everyone stood around him, watching and waiting for some meaningful pronouncement or wise words.

There was a pause. Then the king spoke, addressing the waves, not the people around him.

'As your king, I command you, great ocean,' said Canute to the waves, 'do not move, and do not come in any further. Do not wet my feet, and do not soak my royal robes.'

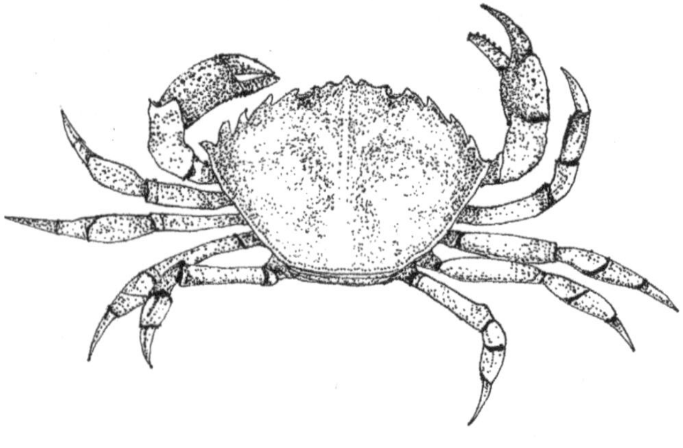

There was another pause, longer this time. There was silence apart from the continued swish of the waves on the shore. Every so often, one wave was bigger than the rest. Eventually, one of the waves soaked the king's feet, his robes, and his legs right up to his knees.

The king laughed, got off his throne and started to walk up the beach, and so everyone followed him. Then he turned around, held out his hand and spoke again.

'Let this be a lesson to all of you. The sea cannot be controlled by the king. The power of kings is empty and worthless. Only the power of God can control the waves. All else is fallible.'

Back at the royal lodgings, Canute hung his golden crown on a crucifix on the wall.

'This I do, in honour of God – the true and almighty king.'

Did Canute ever choose to wear the crown again, when it helped to assert his authority? Probably.

LOST TO THE SEA

England's coastline has always been in a state of change. Our folk tales are full of the shadows and ghosts of land that has been lost to the sea.

Eight thousand years ago, we were cut off from mainland Europe by the rising ocean. Recent research has shown that Doggerland, the connecting land to the east of England, was once a rich landscape where Mesolithic people would hunt, fowl and fish. Once upon a time, the Thames and the Rhine shared the same estuary.

Dogger Bank, the highest area of Doggerland, is now a submerged sand bank about 60 miles from England's east coast. Fans of the Shipping Forecast might like to know that the name comes from a type of medieval fishing boat: Dogger Bank has long been known as a good fishing ground. Significant offshore wind turbine developments are now being built here, to harvest energy rather than fish.

Sea-flooded lands are a more recent phenomenon in England too, right through to the present day. Some are well documented and evidenced, providing fascinating hunting grounds for divers and archaeologists armed with new technology. Others have passed into legend, tangled with stories of heroes and ghosts. They join a great deluge of traditional flood stories from all over the world, going back to Noah's Ark.

The Isles of Scilly lie 24 nautical miles south-west of Cornwall, although anyone who has travelled on the good ship Scillonian III *in bad weather might be forgiven for thinking it's a lot further than that. Scilly is a favourite place of mine: a wonderful landscape and seascape to explore, with incredible wildlife. It's sometimes possible to walk between islands at low tide. On my first visit there, aged about 10, I remember sitting by a labyrinth, looking out to sea, with the robins eating out of my hand.*

Evidence points to more land in the extreme south-west of the British Isles in ancient times, possibly giving rise to the myth of Lyonesse. It's thought that the Isles of Scilly used to be much larger, forming one large island called Ennor *(Cornish for 'great island'), and that the sea gradually rose over centuries until finally the salt marsh in the centre eroded, as late as AD 900. A major archaeological investigation, the Lyonesse Project, has evidenced the transition over millennia from a large island to the pattern of the Isles of Scilly that we know today.*

Some Cornish place names also suggest different boundaries of shore and land. St Michael's Mount near Penzance is translated from the Cornish as 'the grey rock in the wood'. Early medieval writers describe St Michael's Mount as being miles away from the sea in thick woodland, although it's likely that it was inundated over 4,000 years ago.

The Cornish name for Lyonesse is Lethowsow, *derived from the name for the Seven Stone Reef which lies 8 miles north-west of Scilly. It means 'the milky ones', a reference to the constant white water over the area. This reef is a serious hazard for shipping, and the site of an estimated 200 shipwrecks.*

The most famous of these was the supertanker SS Torrey Canyon, *which on 18 March 1967 took a short cut between Scilly and the Seven Stones en route from Kuwait to Milford Haven, carrying a full cargo of crude oil. The ship struck the westerly edge of the Seven Stones, creating an oil slick of 270 square miles – the largest oil spill ever to have occurred in British waters. It contaminated 120 miles of Cornish and 50 miles of French coast, leading to the death of an estimated 15,000 sea birds and much other sea life.*

The story of Lyonesse shares many motifs with the tale of Cantre'r Gwaelod in Wales, and Ys in Brittany. It is impossible to know how much these stories owe to folk memory of the land and sea, and how much they owe to travelling tales. There is also a connection with the story of the Mermaid of Zennor elsewhere in this book, featuring the warning bell of Lyonesse.

Many years ago, water levels were a lot lower than they are today. The old stories tell of a lost land, Lyonesse, somewhere between Scilly and the Cornish coast. Its capital was called the City of Lions, and it had 140 parishes with a watchtower at the sea wall to guide the ships.

The most famous son of Lyonesse was called Tristan, whose father, Meliodas, was the king of Lyonesse during the time of Arthur. Tristan was never able to take up his kingship after the death of his father, because Lyonesse sank beneath the waves in a single night while he was away at his uncle King Mark's court.

On the night Lyonesse disappeared there was a great storm, wilder than anyone had ever known. The winds howled and the waves breached the sea defences, flooding the land. All of Lyonesse was submerged, and everyone perished, apart from one man called Trevelyan.

This man knew how to read the land and read the weather, and that day he woke from sleeping under a tree and saw the great storm approaching. There was no time to lose, and so he didn't bother to saddle his fine white horse; he leapt up and rode bareback, inland to Cornwall, to beat the waves.

But the hungry tide was faster than his horse, and salt water was soon lapping at its hooves. Now the horse was galloping furiously through shallow tides, and now stronger currents as the water deepened, threatening the balance of his steed. Trevelyan held on tight, dug in his heels and bade the horse go even faster, to beat the white sea foam, for he was riding for both their lives.

It wasn't long before the horse was swimming towards the high land of Cornwall. It paced itself and kept going until its feet touched solid ground again. Then that heroic horse could walk both itself and Trevelyan to safety.

As the only survivors of the great storm and the inundation of Lyonesse, Trevelyan's family became great, and the name Trevelyan survives in Cornwall to this day. Their coat of arms shows a white horse rising from the waves in triumph.

If a storm that strong ever approaches Cornwall again (and perhaps one day soon it will), they say that the great bell of Lyonesse will ring out a warning to the people on the coast, so they do not suffer the same sorry fate as the people of Lyonesse. They will be able to outrun the waves in time to save their own lives – and perhaps the lives of some of their animals too.

The east of England is particularly prone to losing land at the coast, especially in low-lying areas around East Anglia. From the Humber to the Thames, the land is sinking by about 5cm every year; in addition, sea levels are predicted to rise up to a metre in the next century. That's particularly worrisome for the area around the Wash and the Norfolk Broads. Elsewhere on the east coast, soft cliffs are vulnerable to rapid erosion from the sea.

Much work is underway all around the English coast to manage coastal erosion and flood risk in a controlled way where possible. Choosing to give land back to sea-flooded saltmarsh may reduce risk in other areas; sometimes hard flood defences may be needed. But the impact of storm surges and high tides is difficult to predict. The terrible North Sea floods of early 1953, which killed over 300 people in the east of England, are still strong in the memory of local communities.

This story tells of a Suffolk city lost to the sea. It was once one of the most important ports in England, but the coast here is now about

2km west of its position in Roman times. The stories of Dunwich are only now coming to light, thanks to local historians, divers and academics who are painstakingly piecing together the details.

Once upon a time, Dunwich was the great capital of East Anglia, the seat of bishops, a thriving port big enough to rival even London. Its harbour was well sheltered from the North Sea. The buildings on the north side of the Dunwich river enjoyed wide, flat vistas across the coast with huge skies; most buildings on the south side of the river were a little higher up on the cliffs.

Dunwich was a city of wonder and riches, with eight churches, a daily market and a bustling port. It had over seventy fishing boats and a naval base. Everyone wanted to come to Dunwich, especially after it was awarded a Royal Charter. Merchants invested their money here, excited by the opportunities for trade in wool, wine and salt, and comforted by the stone walls and great gates that protected the city.

But it was impossible to protect Dunwich from the sea.

In 1286, a massive storm came. The city was overcome with salt water and hurricane-strength winds, cliffs crumbled into the sea, and many houses were lost or wrecked. Two more violent storms followed the next year. The harbour was destroyed and the monastery was swept into the sea.

The good people of Dunwich tried to patch up the damage to their homes. They spent years building a new monastery a little way inland, and new houses to replace the old. But their work was in vain. Time and time again, as soon as they had rebuilt the damage, another storm came to rip it down. The great waves carved chunks out of the cliffs and the sea swallowed up all the low-lying land. In 1362, a violent storm destroyed much of what was left of the old medieval city.

Dunwich was rebuilt yet again; by the 1500s it was a modest town a little further inland. But the sea was greedy. Over the centuries that followed, the sea and the storms swallowed up the town, church by church, bit by bit. The final church to be taken by the sea was All Saints, which tumbled into the sea in 1911. The old stone towers of Dunwich are now the underwater home of sponges and crabs.

Today, Dunwich is now a sleepy one-road village of around 200 people. It boasts a little museum where local people can explore, celebrate and ponder the lost stories of all those who lived on the land nearby – the land that has now become the sea.

Sometimes, the bells of the lost churches of Dunwich can still be heard chiming from their grave under the waves. It's a reminder of the fact that nothing lasts forever.

If sailors hear those bells, they refuse to sail. It means that yet another storm is on the way, and the sea is still hungry.

THE PRESS GANG

It has always been difficult to persuade people into military service, particularly during wartime. Press gangs were employed in England between the sixteenth and nineteenth centuries, usually to force seafaring men into the navy. Press gangs had official sanction and their decisions were upheld in the courts, because a strong navy was important to the security of the realm. By the time of the Battle of Trafalgar, over half of the Royal Navy were pressed men. Impressment was abolished in Britain after the defeat of Napoleon in 1815 at Waterloo. Conscription to the wider military forces has happened repeatedly since that time, of course; it was only abolished in 1960.

All the men who worked the sea and lived at the English coast knew of the threat of the press gang. They knew that the people-snatchers liked to bag a fisherman, because they were already skilled in matters of sailing and the sea and, being at the coast and away from settlements, they were vulnerable. The violent press-gang thugs would snatch young men away, bundle them on to ships to serve in the navy or worse, and the poor victims would often never be heard from again.

This tale of the press gang was recorded in Yorkshire as a true story. Sadly, it also demonstrates how people might use the press gang to their own spiteful ends.

Human trafficking and people smuggling are still happening today on the coasts of England, despite state efforts to prevent them. It is depressing to think that this particularly rancid aspect of human society is still widespread. True stories and witness statements play an important part in exposing such atrocities.

Somewhere between Whitby and Robin Hood's Bay there lived a farmer called Mossburn. He had two strong and pretty daughters, Hester and Dorothy. Those two girls were the secret sweethearts of two brothers, Bill and Peter, who worked in the Greenland fishery.

They'd had a twinkle for each other before the two lads had gone away on their last fishing trip, but the lads were nervous of making their feelings widely known. Farmer Mossburn was quite well-to-do and he would want to secure good futures for both his daughters.

Now the two fishermen brothers had returned, and they'd done well. Each of them had been given responsibility for a boat in the fleet, and been commended for their courage by the owner. Bursting with pride, Bill and Peter decided to go up to the farm as quickly as they could, to share the good news and make things a bit more formal with their beloved girls.

A little way from the town, they bumped into another girl, Polly, walking down the track.

Polly blushed. 'You'll go with me, Billy, will ye?' she said to the younger brother, 'it's been a while since I've seen you.'

Bill was embarrassed at this. He used to laugh and joke with Polly, but that was before he'd met Hester Mossburn.

'Nay, Polly, I cannot go with you – I have another fish to fry,' he said, in a kindly way.

'Not that Hester Mossburn,' said Polly, as if she was spitting.

'Now, Polly,' interrupted Peter, patting Polly on the arm in a fatherly way, 'Bill and Hester are made for each other. All we need to do is set the date. It's not for you to say otherwise.'

Polly wrenched her arm away, and this time she did spit. 'Curse you, Billy. Curses on the both of you.' She ran fast down the hill then. Peter yelled after her, 'Curses always come home to roost,' but she was gone.

That meeting put a dampener on the lads' high spirits, but not for long. When they'd got to the farm, and they saw Hester and Dorothy again after such a long time away, well, the emotions ran high. Words of meaning and of commitment were said, kisses were exchanged, and when old Farmer Mossburn heard the news, he gave his hearty consent to the marriage of Dorothy to Peter, and of Hester to Bill. The lads suggested a speedy marriage before the next fishing voyage, and a date was soon set. The farmhouse was full to overflowing with joy.

It was dusk by the time the two brothers took their leave, and the lovers wanted private time to say goodbye. So first Peter and Dorothy went out of the farmhouse to kiss their lingering farewells.

Inside the farmhouse, the girls' mother looked up and tutted. 'They've been a while,' she said.

Suddenly the door flew open, and in came Dorothy, pale-faced and shrieking, 'T' press gang! They've got Peter fast!'

Both Farmer Mossburn and Bill rushed out to deal with the press-gang thugs, and what a mistake that was. Farmer Mossburn was felled to the ground with a single blow, and young Bill was bundled up and carried away to take his place beside his brother in the press gang's little boat. By the time he came round, all three women wailing their lament, Farmer Mossburn couldn't remember anything.

Months passed, and news of the wars came, but every battle and every victory was a grief to the Mossburn girls, as they feared for their sweethearts' lives. As time went by, both girls wore mourning dresses.

As for Polly, she carried on her work sorting the fish that the fishing fleets brought in. One day, she boasted to those round and about at the local fish market, 'If a lad breaks faith with me, I'll punish him and he'll be sorry for it. Just ask Hester Mossburn.'

There was a stunned silence all around her.

An old fisherman grabbed her arm. 'Are ye false, young Polly? I didn't think such a one could live among us.' He flung Polly to the ground, and nobody came forward to help.

Polly gathered herself and her skirts up off the stones with a scowl, but all the faces around her were cold and accusing. Of course, somewhere deep down inside Polly was feeling guilty, and scared of vengeance. She ran from that place, and never dared to show her face again.

The story spread like a plague around the villages on the coast. Polly's landlady turned her out of her lodgings, and nobody would give her work or shelter. Polly was outcast: the one who had betrayed Whitby sailors to the press gang. At last she went crazy, wandering out on the moors, the wild elements taking away her reason.

Meanwhile, Dorothy and Hester Mossburn waited, and waited, for four long years. They would have waited more, but one day their Peter and Bill stood in front of them once again, alive but seriously wounded from war. For all four of them, their joy was mixed with grief.

There was eventually a double wedding, but the story doesn't say if they were happy ever after.

Grace Darling

In the whirlwind year of 1838, the year of Queen Victoria's coronation, the first railways were being built across England and Charles Dickens published his novel Oliver Twist. *Many young women were still aspiring to behave like one of Jane Austen's heroines. Nevertheless, in November 1838 a 5ft 2in, 22-year-old lass from Northumberland became a celebrated sea hero. The name of Grace Darling has swirled around the centuries since that time, synonymous with sea rescue in England.*

Although lifeboats existed at the time of Grace Darling's daring heroism, they have developed apace since Victorian times. The Royal National Lifeboat Institution (RNLI) now protects coastlines all around Britain and Ireland. In 2024, it operates a twenty-four-hour search and rescue service all year round, with 238 lifeboat stations and a fleet of over 400 lifeboats. Since 1824, when it was founded, the RNLI has saved over 144,000 lives and they still take Grace Darling as their inspiration. These brave and dedicated men and women deserve our support.

Here is a true story that takes pride of place in England's marine folklore. It's not a tale of doom or warning. It tells of selflessness and practical quick thinking to help others.

It was 1838. Grace Darling lived with her father, mother, four brothers and four sisters in Longstone Lighthouse on a small island of the Northumbrian coast.

Even though the lighthouse was new, it was basic. There was one large room with a stove for heating, and a spiral staircase that led up to three bedrooms, with the light above all of them. They had to row over to the next of the Farne Islands regularly to fetch supplies, to grow vegetables and to feed the animals.

After a run of very cold winters, 1838's summer weather had been disappointing and September had already brought the first frosts inland. On the night of 7 September, a storm raged around the lighthouse.

Grace couldn't sleep. At just after 4 a.m. she looked out of her bedroom window and saw the wreck of a steamship, the *Forfarshire*, foundering on the rocks about a mile away. Half of the boat had already sunk. Grace watched as the light of a new day came up in the east. Then, with the telescope, she could make out the shapes of survivors crawling on to the rocks. The weather was too rough for the lifeboat to help.

Grace and her father William decided to act then. They took their little rowing boat out in appalling conditions, one oar each, and rowed almost a mile to avoid being wrecked on the rocks themselves. Then William managed to get from the boat to the rocks where the survivors were huddled, leaving Grace to manage the little wooden boat on her own.

There were nine survivors from the wreck of the *Forfarshire*, eight men (one badly injured) and one woman (holding her two children, who had already died of exposure). It took two boat trips in worsening tides and storms for Grace and William to rescue the living and bring them back to the lighthouse. They stayed there in warmth and safety for the next three days, before the weather would allow them to access the mainland.

The rescue made headline news around the world – and it was Grace, the unlikely heroine, who got all the attention. She became an early Victorian celebrity, lauded in the newspapers, depicted in paintings and praised in poems. Queen Victoria sent £50 as a token of her gratitude, and the Duke of Northumberland appointed himself as Grace's guardian to help her manage her new-found status as national heroine.

None of this impressed Grace very much. She was shy and hated the limelight, so the endless responding to letters and requests for locks of hair were all too much for her. As far as she was concerned, she and her father had just done the right thing.

Grace died four years later from tuberculosis, at the age of 26, but her name and her inspiration lives on. It is possible to visit her grave at St Aiden's church in Bamburgh, Northumberland.

OTHER WORLDS

What is this strange phenomenon called the sea? People of earlier times did not have access to the scientific information about the sea that we enjoy, and even our modern knowledge of the deep ocean is incomplete. Many folk tales from earlier centuries ponder on the possibility of marine otherworlds, both under and over the ocean. They tell of people with magical powers who could access these places and be at ease there – or even prefer it to our reality.

My first example of such a tale comes from the Isle of Man, recorded by George Waldron in 1726. It concerns another world altogether beneath the waves. Stories of people who could survive and breathe underwater are frequently found across the British Isles from times before scuba diving, although mermen seem to lack the tails of their female counterparts.

The last tale in this collection is a very ancient and strange story from the English cleric Gervase of Tilbury's Otia Imperialia *in 1211. Sightings of worlds in the sky that appear over the sea are very common across England and beyond. Sabine Baring-Gould mused that they reflect the ancient notion of a 'ship of souls' in the clouds, or a whole community in the sky that poured down rain and storms to the earth, and plundered its resources. He also makes a connection to the Norse tradition of a 'rainbow bridge' between the land of the gods and Middle-Earth. Others have interpreted these curiosities as cloud formations, mirages or … who knows, perhaps even rare sightings of other planes of existence.*

It's a fittingly Neptunian way to end this folk tale journey with England's coasts and seas. As the world changes, we may abuse, manage, or even try to ignore the vast salt water that defines our islands. But ultimately, the great ocean around us is still unfathomable and mysterious. It will show us what it chooses.

A great project was created in the late seventeenth century, to seek treasures in the sea. Several ships were commissioned, each kitted out with great glass jars cased in tough leather, big enough to carry a person. These were meant to carry divers who would be lowered down to the seabed to search. They could be retrieved quickly to the surface, so that divers could gulp the air before continuing.

One of these ships travelled to the Isle of Man. The owners knew the history of this wonderful place and hoped to find lost treasures scattered in the seas around. A man was let down from the ship in his glass and leather machine, on a stout rope.

But the rope kept on descending, fathoms and fathoms down, until it nearly ran out, and had to be tied to the ship for fear of losing it. Those on the ship were concerned, and so the rope was wound back up again on its great wheel. Finally, the man reappeared at the surface in his container, still alive, but clearly distressed.

'I wish the rope had been longer!' he cried. 'If I had but travelled a little further, I could have landed there, and I could have stayed.'

On further questioning by all those gathered around, the man told them that after he had travelled through shoals of fish, he had come to a 'pure element' clear as air, towards the seabed which was paved with coral and glittering pebbles. There were large streets and squares, made of mother of pearl and decorated with exquisite crystals, and through the windows of the buildings he could see the shimmer of gold and the glistening of gems. He had reached out his hand, but the rope had proved too short to allow him to grasp any treasure.

'Then,' he said mournfully, 'mer-people came, frightened at the sight of me. I tried to speak to them, and found I could breathe quite easily, but then you wound the rope back in and they were lost to me.'

In the days that followed, the man's melancholy grew. Dissatisfied at human life above the waves and completely inconsolable, he died a few days later.

One Sunday, on a feast day somewhere in England, the congregation came streaming out of the church, glad the sermon was over and looking forward to Sunday lunch. But they were to witness a true miracle.

'Look! Look up there!' cried a young woman.

From the clouds above them, an anchor was descending, attached to a stout rope. Unfortunately, the metal met the earth on one of the graves, and whoever was above the clouds tugged it taut; this made the anchor secure itself on the solid granite of the gravestone. The rope was shaken and shaken by somebody, but the anchor would not loosen.

The gaping congregation on the ground then heard voices from above the clouds, discussing what to do. 'Send someone down to release the anchor!' said a clear voice. There was general agreement from the people above the clouds.

Then a sailor appeared, deftly climbing down the rope.

The sailor looked about him wildly. He appeared to be struggling to breathe, as if he was drowning in the heavy atmosphere below the cloud. He gasped, collapsed, and fell to the ground as if dead; yet nobody dared to go near him. The congregation just watched, afraid, and waited to see what would happen next.

After about half an hour, those in the vessel above the clouds cut the rope and it fell to the earth. We don't know what happened to the sailor, or the rope.

The only other part of this tale that has survived the test of time is the detail of how the anchor's metal was used (waste not, want not). It was hammered out into the hinges and door furniture of the church door, where, apparently, they were still to be seen in 1211.

Unfortunately, the story doesn't tell us which particular parish in England was blessed with such a miracle.

STORY SOURCES AND FURTHER READING

Alexander, M., *The Earliest English Poems* (Penguin, 1966)

Anonymous, *Legends of Devon* (London: Whittaker and Company, Exeter: Holden-Wallis, Dawlish LA Westcott, 1848)

Anonymous, *Smuggling & Smugglers in Sussex: The Genuine History of the Inhuman and Unparalleled Murders of Mr. William Galley a Custom-house Officer, and Mr. Daniel Chater, a Shoemaker, by Fourteen Notorious Smugglers, with the Trials and Execution of Seven of the Criminals at Chichester, 1748–9* (W.J. Smith, 1900, derived from 1749)

Bacon, J., and Bacon, S., *The Search for Dunwich: City Under the Sea* (Segment, 1979)

Baring-Gould, S., *A Book of Folk-Lore* (Collins, 1913)

Baring-Gould, S., *Devonshire Characters and Strange Events* (John Lane, 1908)

Baring-Gould, S., *The Vicar of Morwenstow* (London: Henry S. King, 1876)

Blakeborough, R., *Wit, Character, Folklore and Customs of the North Riding of Yorkshire* (London: H. Frowde, 1898)

Bottrell, W., *Traditions and Hearthside Stories of West Cornwall, First Series* (W. Cornish, for the author, 1870)

Bottrell, W., *Traditions and Hearthside Stories of West Cornwall, Second Series* (Penzance, England: Beare and Son, 1873)

Bray, A.E., *Legends, Superstitions, and Sketches of Devonshire on the Borders of the Tamar and the Tavy, Illustrative of its Manners, Customs, History, Antiquities, Scenery, and Natural History*, vol. 2 (London: Newman 1844)

Briggs, K., *A Dictionary of British Folk Tales* (Routledge and Kegan Paul, 1971)

Briggs, K., *A Dictionary of Fairies: Hobgoblins, Brownies, Bogies and Other Supernatural Creatures* (Allen Lane, 1976)

Briggs, K., and Tongue, R.L., *Folktales of England* (University of Chicago Press, 1965)

Charlton, L., *The History of Whitby and Whitby Abbey* (1779)

Charman, D., Johns, C., Camidge, K., Marshall, P., Mills, S.F., Mulville, J., Roberts, H.M., *The Lyonesse Project: A Study of the Coastal and Marine Environment of the Isles of Scilly* (OASIS ID cornwall2-58903), https://doi.org/10.5284/1025045, (York: Archaeology Data Service, 2014)

Child, F.J., *English and Scottish Popular Ballads* (Boston: Houghton Mifflin Co., 1905)

Clover, C., *Rewilding the Sea* (Witness, 2022)

Coleridge, S.T., *The Poems of Samuel Taylor Coleridge* (Oxford University Press, 1921)

Coxhead, J.R.W., *The Devil in Devon: An Anthology of Folk Tales* (West Country Handbooks, 1967)

Cunningham, H., *Grace Darling: Victorian Heroine* (Hambledon, 2007)

Dacre, M., *Devonshire Folk Tales* (The History Press, 2010)

Deane, T., and Shaw, T., *Folklore of Cornwall* (The History Press, 2003)

Dickens, C., *The Uncommercial Traveller* (London: Chapman and Hall, 1861)

Dinsdale, T., *The Leviathans* (Routledge & Kegan Paul, 1966)

Dobson, R.B., and Taylor, J., *Rymes of Robin Hood: An Introduction to the English Outlaw* (William Heinemann, 1976)

Downes, J., *The Owlman and Others* (CFZ Publications, 1997)

Farr, G.E., *Smuggling in North Devon* (Unpublished, undated)

Feinstein, Elaine, *Lawrence's Women: The Intimate Life of D.H. Lawrence* (Harper Collins, 1993)

Fisk, S., *Abandoned Communities: Dunwich*, www.abandonedcommunities.co.uk/page11.html

Forbes, A., (Rev. Forbes Phillips) *The Romance of Smuggling* (Pearson, 1909)

Gardner, T., *An Historical Account of Dunwich, antiently a city, now a borough; Blithburgh, formerly a town of note, now a village; Southwold, once a village, now a town-corporate; with remarks on some places contiguous thereto* (London: 1754)

Gervase of Tilbury, *Otia Imperialia (Recreation for an Emperor)*, ed. and trans. S.E. Banks and J.W. Binns (Clarendon Press, 2002)

Gill, W.W., *A Manx Scrapbook* (London & Bristol: 1929)

Green, L., *The Astrological Neptune and the Quest for Redemption* (Samuel Weiser, 1996)

Grice, F., *Folk Tales of the North Country* (Nelson, 1944)

Hartland, E.S., *English Fairy and other Folk Tales* (London: W. Scott, 1906)

Hasted, E., *The History and Topographical Survey of the County of Kent: Volume 5* (Canterbury: W. Bristow, 1798)

Heddon-on-the-Wall Local History Society, *The Laidley Worm of Spindlestone Heugh*, http://heddonhistory.weebly.com/blog/the-laidley-worm-of-spindlestone-heugh (29 March 2015)

Henderson, W., *Notes on the Folk-Lore of the Northern Counties of England and of the Borders* (London: W. Satchell, Peyton & Co., 1879)

Hunt, R., *Popular Romances of the West of England; or, The Drolls, Traditions, and Superstitions of Old Cornwall* (3rd ed.) (Chatto and Windus, 1903)
Hutchinson, W., *The History & Antiquities of the County Palatine of Durham* (Mr S. Hodgson and Messrs Robinsons, 1785)
Igglesden, C., *A Saunter through Kent with Pen and Pencil*, vol. 1 (Ashford, Kent: Published at the Offices of the *Kentish Express*, 1925)
Jacobs, J., *English Fairy Tales* (David Nutt, 1890)
Jacobs, J., *More English Fairy Tales* (David Nutt, 1894)
James, R.M., Morgawr and the Folkloresque: (A study of a whopping fish tale). *Shima*, vol. 16(2), pp. 160–72 (2022)
Kingshill, S., and Westwood, J., *The Fabled Coast: Legends and Traditions from Around the Shores of Britain and Ireland* (Random House, 2010)
Kipling, R., *Puck of Pook's Hill* (Macmillan and Co., 1906)
Marine Climate Change Impacts Partnership (MCCIP), *Impacts hub* www.mccip.org.uk/all-uk/uk-impacts/hub (2024 and updated)
Marine Management Organisation, *UK Sea Fisheries Statistics 2022* https://assets.publishing.service.gov.uk/media/654e277cce0b3a000d491530/UK_Sea_Fisheries_Statistics_2022_101123.pdf (2013)
Marshall, S., *Everyman's Book of English Folk Tales* (Dent, 1981)
Moore, H.T. (ed.), *The Collected Letters of D.H. Lawrence*, vol. 1 (Heinemann, London, 1970)
Morris, M., *The Anglo-Saxons: A History of the Beginnings of England* (Hutchinson, 2021)
Morton Nance, R., 'Tom Bawcock's Eve', *Journal of Old Cornwall*, vol. 5, pp. 20–22 (1927) and version courtesty of Cornish National Music Archive, https://cornishnationalmusicarchive.co.uk/content/tom-bawcocks-eve/
Norway, A.H., *Highways and Byways in Yorkshire* (Joseph Pennell and Hugh Thomson, 1903)
O'Connor, M., *Cornish Folk Tales* (The History Press, 2010)
Parkinson, T., *Yorkshire Traditions and Legends* (London: 1889)
Phillip, N. (ed.), *The Penguin Book of English Folk Tales* (Penguin, 1992)
Platt, R., *Smuggler's Britain.* Website resource at www.smuggling.co.uk
Platt, R., *Smuggling in the British Isles: A History* (The History Press, 2012)
Pringle, P., *The Pegasus Book of Smugglers* (Dennis Dobson, 1965)
RNLI, *What we do.* RNLI website https://rnli.org/what-we-do (2024)
Robson, J.P. (ed.), *Songs of the Bards of the Tyne* (P. France & Co., 1849)
Rollinson, W., *Cumbrian Dictionary of Dialect, Tradition and Folklore* (Otley, 1997)
Simeon of Durham, trans. Rev. Joseph Stevenson, *The Historical Works of Simeon of Durham* (London: 1855)
Suffling, E., *History and Legends of the Broad District* (Jarrold, 1896)
Thompson, T.W., 'English Gypsy Folk-Tales and other Traditional Stories', *Journal of the Gypsy Lore Society*, new series, vol. 8 (1914–15)

Tongue, R., *Forgotten Folk Tales of the English Counties* (Routledge & Kegan Paul, 1970)
University of Bradford, *Europe's Lost Frontiers*, www.bradford.ac.uk/archaeological-forensic-sciences/research/europes-lost-frontiers/ (2024)
Waddell, H., *Beasts and Saints* (London: Constable, 1934)
Waldron, G., *A Description of the Isle of Man* (Douglas: 1865, reprint of 1731 text)
Westwood, J., and Simpson, J., *The Lore of the Land: A Guide to England's Legends from Spring-Heeled Jack to the Witches of Warboys* (Penguin, 2005)
Yates, D.E., *Gypsy Folk-Tales* (Phoenix House, 1948)